Facing the Hunchback of Notre Dame

the Enchanted Attic

BOOK ONE

Facing the Hunchback of Notre Dame

L.L. SAMSON

ZONDERVAN.com/
AUTHORTRACKER
follow your favorite authors

ZONDERKIDZ

Facing the Hunchback of Notre Dame
Copyright © 2012 by L. L. Samson

This title is also available as a Zondervan ebook.

Requests for information should be addressed to:
Zonderkidz, *Grand Rapids, Michigan* 49530

Library of Congress Cataloging-in-Publication Data

Samson, Lisa, 1964-
    Facing the hunchback of Notre Dame / by Lisa Samson.
       p.   cm. — (The enchanted attic ; bk. 1)
    Summary: When Quasimodo from Victor Hugo's "The Hunchback of Notre
Dame" appears fully alive and completely bewildered in their attic, twin twelve-
year-old avid readers Ophelia and Linus search for a way to help him return home.
    ISBN 978-0-310-72795-8 (softcover)
    [1. Space and time—Fiction. 2. Characters in literature—Fiction. 3. Hugo,
Victor, 1802-1885. Hunchback of Notre Dame—Fiction. 4. Books and reading—
Fiction. 5. Brothers and sisters—Fiction. 6. Twins—Fiction.] I. Title.
PZ7.S1697Fac 2012
[E]—dc23   2011048879

Cover design: Kris Nelson
Cover and interior illustrations: ©Antonio Caparo
Interior design: Ben Fetterley & Sherri L. Hoffman

Printed in the United States of America

12 13 14 15 16 17 /DCI/ 26 25 24 23 22 21 20 19 18 17 16 15 14 13 12 11 10 9 8 7 6 5 4 3 2

Contents

prologue

What You Need to Know Before Reading This Fantastic Little Book ...

Or All of This Backstory Isn't Normally a Good Idea, but We'd Like to Get On with Things

ackstory: The past events leading up to the present story so the reader might better understand the current happenings.

The adventures began when fourteen-year-old twins Linus and Ophelia Easterday were deserted by their parents. Drs. Antonia and Ron Easterday (PhD, of course) never thought much about anyone other than themselves and their lepidoptera (four-winged insects such as butterflies and moths). So for this reason they have no problem leaving their children in the care of Portia and Augustus Sandwich, the kids' aunt and uncle on their mother's side, also twins. And on this particular excursion, they were scheduled to be gone for at least five years. Five years! How could they leave their children behind for such a length of time?

The children bade their parents good-bye at the docks in New York City, as Ron and Antonia set out on a boat called *The Basset Hound* to study never-before-seen butterflies on the island of Willis, which was discovered by Willis Cranston from Ho-Ho-Kus, New Jersey, while parasailing from a cruise ship. That is all we know about Mr. Cranston, and most likely that's all we should know about him.

Both children were actually a bit relieved at Antonia and Ron's departure, due to the fact that the Drs. Easterday are lousy parents. Therefore, the children had grown up primarily on peanut butter and jelly sandwiches, cold cereal, and instant oatmeal. And not even the most delightful peaches and cream kind, I might add. Plus, they'd been doing their own laundry for more than seven years now. A crime! Hopefully your parents are much worthier than those two. If not, you have my most sincere condolences (feelings of pity while wishing circumstances could be better for you, even though they cannot).

Linus and Ophelia, enjoying the carefree lifestyle that is summer vacation, hopped aboard a train and headed inland for the town of Kingscross, where the esteemed Kingscross University has been educating minds since the late 1600s. Snow and ice regularly occur during a Kingscross wintertime, and I've watched a colleague or two of mine in the English department fall down flat on the steps leading into our building. May I admit that I chuckled?

They do not respect me here at the university, but who cleans up the messes of their infernal making? It is I, Bartholomew Inkster, that's who. Of course, they look down their noses at me because I've never had the time, what with having a real job and all, to earn the number of degrees that they have. But let's face facts: If you were given the choice between having either all of the janitors or all of the English professors in the world disappear, who would go first? My point exactly! And if I laid my reading list alongside any one of theirs, guess whose would be longer and more diverse? That's right. You guessed it.

The children eventually arrived at their aunt and uncle's home on Rickshaw Street. Portia and Augustus Sandwich live in a townhouse three stories tall and built from stone the color of verdigris (the green that collects on copper). The bottom floor of the Sandwiches's townhome holds the family business, Seven Hills Better Books, which sells rare and antiquarian books. In other words, either there aren't many of these volumes left, or they smell like mildew. Portia runs the place, and she always offers me a peppermint whenever I enter the shop to peruse the current findings.

But beware: while in their shop, I've occasionally witnessed shifting shadows, a hint of cloak, a waft of odor ... only to turn around quickly and find nothing there. Just a little warning, mind. Nobody else seems to notice these things, and I hate to bring it up at the risk of ruining Portia's business.

Augustus, when not at auctions looking for ancient merchandise, sits around and talks with the customers—mostly about twaddle, but everyone needs to chat about insignificant topics on a regular basis. It clears the mind for more important matters.

Portia and Augustus are brother and sister. I believe I mentioned previously that they are twins as well, and they secretly believe the Drs. Easterday are loony to leave behind such adorable children. I do have to wonder, however, if Linus and Ophelia behave better for their aunt and uncle than they do for their parents. It's just a suspicion and clearly I might be mistaken. The children have always seemed most polite when I've encountered them in the store.

The bookstore has been in place for almost two decades, yet the older residents of Rickshaw Street remember when Cato Grubbs owned the house. He ran an apothecary and laboratory equipment shop—and a rather successful one at that—until he mysteriously disappeared. One day he was there serving his customers, and the next day his shop door remained locked. Not a single person saw him leave. He said good-bye to no one.

Eventually the bank regained ownership of the building until Augustus and Portia obtained it at quite the bargain. As such, the bank did not pay to have Cato's belongings removed, which is how the younger set of twins came to suspect that Cato did much more than sell beakers and burners. They do have quite an overactive imagination, those two. They'd been living with Augustus and Portia for about a month when they discovered their suspicions held weight (a thousand pounds worth).

Why don't Linus and Ophelia tell this story themselves? Easy. Not just anyone can write a piece of fiction! Linus is scientific, and Ophelia dissects novels a bit too much to get taken up in the writing of one. So they asked me, Bartholomew Inkster, to tell it for them because I know my way around a pen and some paper, and also because I believe their story is worth telling. That's the most important qualification, after all.

Before you continue on, I would like to explain a few things so you may be an informed reader. Being a self-educated, literary fussbudget (a needlessly fault-finding person), it is within my nature to explain a bit of the writing process as I proceed. You may choose to either use these tidbits of information to increase your knowledge of English and the fine art of writing, or ignore the opportunity to learn literary technique from an expert and simply skip over my explanations. If you choose to ignore the input that I have so generously provided regarding the writing craft, then you may also choose to ignore the simplified definitions of some of the rather advanced words I've used within the story—words that I've explained at the request of Linus, who seems to think my vocabulary rather too advanced for the average reader. For those who wish to increase their knowledge, read on. For those who prefer to ignore my teachings, well ... read on anyway.

one

Bottles, Books, and Beakers

Or Introducing the Setting and the Main Characters

*W*hen Ophelia Easterday discovered the secret doorway, her brother Linus pretended he'd never seen it before. If anything bad should happen, he figured Ophelia might as well feel responsible too. And Linus didn't want to hurt her feelings. As his twin sister, she was prone to believe he told her everything. He certainly didn't want her to think any differently. Secrets do come in handy at times.

"You've got to see the attic, Linus. It's fantastic!"

They stood in Uncle Augustus's collection room on the second floor, where gowns and costumes from days gone by (organized by time period and fabric) hung in plastic bags on racks, all around the room.

Ophelia moved aside a red velvet curtain to reveal what looked like a plumber's big foul-up. Chunks of plaster were missing, wood laths peered through the holes, and a musty draft breathed over them. But if one pressed against the rightmost protrusion, a door opened without a sound. Ophelia pressed the spot.

"I thought there was a window under here. Imagine my surprise!"

Imagine, Linus thought.

"Look, steps! And you're never going to believe what's up there!"

A mad scientist's lab? Linus thought.

11

As you can see, my dears, Ophelia does a lot of talking while Linus does a lot of thinking. Not that Ophelia doesn't think. Oh no. She is quite bright. Just as bright as Linus, in the IQ sense. However, Linus possesses mathematical smarts as well as practical smarts, which come in handy more often than Ophelia cares to admit. He is very handy around the house as well, and if you need a computer desk assembled, Linus is your man. But don't be too hard on Ophelia. She would give you the shirt off her back. *(That's what we call a cliché, a word or phrase that is tired out, used by millions, and should never be found in the pages of a well-written book. I only included it here so as to alert you to such things used in the books of other writers. I go all around Robin Hood's barn to avoid them like the plague.)*

Linus and Ophelia carefully ascended the dark, narrow staircase.

"Look—it's a lab!" Ophelia burst into the room, her head now level with the slanted planes of the ceiling. You know how attics are.

Linus bent down a bit to fit through the small door. For a boy his age, his height, one could say, seemed a bit showy. And although he and Ophelia tore into the delicate fabric of society only minutes apart, they resembled one another not at all. Her dark, curly head came to the middle of Linus's chest, and he looked down upon her with bright blue eyes beneath a head of straight blond hair. Linus described the two of them as the troll and the princess, while Ophelia argued, "Oh no. We're Lennie and George from *Of Mice and Men.*" This claim always made Linus roll his eyes. *(You will have to read that book in high school, and then you will understand why Linus would rather be a troll.)*

The lab would have made anybody stare with open mouth, which is what both twins had done when they first saw it. Yet now upon their second entry into the attic, they stared open-mouthed again. The room affects people like that. I know I felt the same way the first time I entered the dimly lit space that smells of old shoes, horsehair, hot dogs, and geraniums. Shelves line the front and back walls where vials and bottles and baskets are neatly arranged and labeled. Ginger. Cardamom. Pekoe.

Linus pulled out a basket, his fingers searching through odd bits of junk, most of it very old and seemingly workaday. Nuts, bolts, hinges, nails, bits of fabric, leather, Popsicle sticks, and silver cutlery.

I could do a lot with this stuff, he thought.

"Look at these bottles, Linus!" Ophelia touched another shelf. The bottles held liquids that glowed from the single beam of sunlight streaming through the small window above their heads. One bottle, pyramid shaped with a cork stopper, emitted a variety of colors at the same time! "I wonder what this one's for?"

Linus shook his head. Boy, would he like to find out! In some ways he was annoyed that his sister had also found the attic. Now he was responsible to someone else for whatever happened when he got his hands on these things. Could he, Linus, be a mad scientist in the making?

On one shelf three glass jars—simply labeled One, Two, and Three—sat next to a mortar and pestle. Mandatory scientific apparatus complete with tubes, beakers, and burners rested under a thick layer of dust on a table near the entrance.

Linus suggested that I explain some of the more unusual items in the room. So if you already know what a mortar and pestle are, please forgive me. I do not mean to insult your intelligence. However, for the rest of you, a mortar is a small but heavy bowl, usually made of stone, with thick walls; and the pestle is basically a thick stick with a rounded end that's not only easy to hold, but also fits perfectly in the bowl. With a pestle one might grind seeds or herbs against the inside of the mortar to create a fine powder.

They ran their hands along stacks of ancient books with names like Bringing the Imaginary to Life: A Proposition; Trapdoors to Other Realms; Simple Chemistry to Wow Your Simple Friends (They'll Think You're a Magician!); The History of Alchemy; Physics for Nincompoops; Mixing It Up with Common Chemicals; and Stage Presence—Stage Presents: The Art of Showing Up and Showing Off. Many more books, albeit older and smellier, were written in German; some were written in an alphabet of which even I don't know the origin. These last books were, naturally, the most threadbare and obscure (unknown by most people), and they were also the most apt to send chills down your spine. I'd recommend leaving them alone. "What you do not know will not hurt you" is a widely accepted maxim (old saying, a general truth). Some things really are better left alone, but I also believe that to remain in ignorance can come back to harm you.

"This is a great place to read," Ophelia said as she plopped down on a large, blue velvet couch in the middle of the room. The cushion exhaled a large puff of dust, which was illuminated by the meek shaft of light coming through the dirty window above. Not that any of that dust and grime bothered these children, amazingly enough. "We need to keep this place a secret."

Uh ... yeah, Linus thought.

"Auggie and Portia will think it's too dangerous for us to be up here. And look at that circle painted on the floor." The lip of the circle ended just inches from the couch. "I wonder what that's about?"

Linus did too. He also wondered where that large square bottle of amber liquid that was now sitting on the floor between the couch and the bookcase had come from—and when? It wasn't there before.

"Did you bring that up here?" Linus asked Ophelia.

"No. Did you?"

He shook his head.

Her eyebrows raised. "Really?"

"I swear."

Aunt Portia called to the twins from downstairs, but the words merely tiptoed to them as through a thick fog, "Time for tea!"

"We'll figure out what that bottle is later," Ophelia said as they turned to leave. "We're assuming Uncle Auggie doesn't know anything about this place—but he might. Remember, not a word."

Linus nodded. Some things went without saying.

two

The Gaggle of Rickshaw Street

Or Introducing the Relatives and
Other Secondary, Though Critical Characters

Ophelia pleasantly saw herself and Linus as junior editions of Uncle Augustus and Aunt Portia, destined for a similar existence. Yet Linus stayed awake some nights dreading the very same thing!

You'll like Auggie and Portia. Everybody likes them. They possess that general air of goodwill and, even better, humor. They are actually the aunt and uncle of the twins' mother, Antonia Easterday, who recently wrote a letter to her children full of details about hers and Ron's studies on Willis island, but she never once asked how they were faring in Kingscross. The outrage!

While Linus and Ophelia display almost no physical similarities (other than their toes), Portia and Augustus resemble one another the way a salt shaker resembles a pepper shaker, excepting for the obvious detail of gender. They both stand tall and straight while holding their slim ribcages aloft. And they both possess that soft, dripping candle wax variety of skin that vibrates a bit when they talk. Which is often. Quite the chatty, social pair, they are what one would call extroverts. (An extrovert is a person who becomes energized around other people. Introverts are their opposite—people who recharge by themselves.)

Portia resembles a movie star grown old, her face lovely and gentle, her eyes bright. In other words, she hasn't "let herself go." (Grown-ups say that about older women who gain weight and stop wearing makeup and doing their hair as they age. There are no correlating expressions for men who do the same sort of things.)

"Come sit down." Aunt Portia set the final fork on the chrome-legged table. Then she straightened up and threw her bright blue feather boa over her left shoulder and out of the way.

We're not British, thought Linus, as he did every teatime. *Why not simply call it supper and leave it at that?*

The kitchen, painted a horrifying mustard color with turquoise cabinets, was located on the second floor of the family home. The twins now sat on two of the six antique dining chairs, placed bright pink cloth napkins on their laps, and waited patiently to eat as Aunt Portia passed around potato pancakes, mashed potatoes, and potato salad. *The poor dear has never quite understood that variety in a meal means ingredients, not just preparation.* Her apricot hair, styled in a large wavy coiffure (hairdo) around her face, shivered with each movement. And she'd placed a tiara on top for good measure. *A real diamond tiara, word has it. Where she obtained it, nobody knows. And Portia refuses to say. Good for her. A woman needs a few secrets.*

"We're having a party next week," Portia said as she stabbed a piece of potato salad with her fork. The twins also began eating (to the delight of potato farmers everywhere). "We're calling it 'Medieval Knight Fever.'"

Oh dear. She's rather corny, isn't she? But don't blame her. The name was Auggie's idea. Portia sticks to the classic movies.

Portia continued, "I'm going to need your help. Would you help me serve the food?"

"And we'll need you to dress fifteenth-century French. I have just the items," said Augustus as he joined them, arranging his poplin suit just so. He rearranged his silverware to perfection, then picked up the fork.

What I just described about Augustus is known as telling detail. It reveals something about a character without coming out and describing it with exact words (in this case Uncle Augustus is overly neat and somewhat of a perfectionist. You should see his room. I've been in hospital chambers with more joi de vivre. (Joi de vivre is a French term that means "joy of living.")

"I just saw a copy of *The Hunchback of Notre Dame!*" Ophelia crowed. "I'll start reading it right away in preparation."

"Good girl," Portia beamed. She loved books as much as Ophelia did. "After you're done with it, I'll pass along the book I'm reading now—*The Mill on the Floss* by George Eliot."

A snoozer if I've ever read one. Hopefully you won't be forced to read it too.

"And as for you, Linus," Augustus said, "I need you to construct a fake set of stocks for pictures. It'll be a stitch."

Linus nodded. *Now that I can do.* He cleared his throat. "We heard there was a scientist living here at one time."

"Oh yes!" said Portia. "Cato Grubbs. Mad! They say he conducted crazy experiments in the attic."

"The attic?" asked Ophelia, trying to put as innocent an expression on her face as possible.

Uncle Augustus cleared his throat and set down his fork in the three o'clock position. He wiped his mouth on a napkin and said, "Funny thing, though. We can't find the entrance to the attic. He must have sealed it up when he left."

The adults explained the mysterious circumstances surrounding the scientist's disappearance.

"Is he dead or alive?" asked Linus.

"Nobody knows. At least not around here," said Portia.

A shadow darkened the tablecloth, cast by the body of Mr. Birdwistell who lived above the clock repair shop next door.

Birdwistell is really his name, I assure you. Sometimes writers employ names to further characterization, meaning it helps the reader know the character better. Sometimes the names fit perfectly (read any Charles Dickens book and you'll see what I mean); sometimes they're the opposite of what they really should be. Mr. Birdwistell (pronounced "bird whistle") should have been named Mr. Sharpthistle or Mr. Snakehissle or some such uncomfortable variety of name, for he was more prickly than a yard full of blackberry bushes and meaner than any snake you're likely to come across in your comfortable, boring lifestyle.

Birdwistell tapped the tabletop and harrumphed, "Well, Augustus, it's time for cards at Ronda's. She's making rumaki (bacon wrapped around water chestnuts and baked in a barbecue sauce) and stuffed celery. Are you going to sit there all evening or might we make our way?" A squat man, Dr. Birdwistell teaches philosophy at Kingscross University, and ... well, I hate to tale bear (gossip), but he's gained a terrible reputation for grading arbitrarily. (In other words, he'll give you good grades if he likes you.)

Plus, he thought the twins nuisances—as evidenced by the way he ignored them as they sat eating their tea. Or dinner. Or supper.

Ophelia smiled at him, but he returned her effort with only a condescending grimace.

Then, without warning, Linus's glass of milk tipped over onto Mr. Birdwistell's shoes.

"Oh no!" cried Opehlia, leaning down to clean the polished wing tip with her napkin.

"Clumsy!" Mr. Birdwistell pointed at Linus. "Augustus, you should have a firmer hand with these two. A firmer hand, I say."

Ophelia looked up at Linus and winked.

The gentlemen left, both lighting up pipes as they walked up the street, and the twins were then expected to clean up the "tea things" (or "the supper dishes," as Linus thought of them), while Portia headed out to attend a lecture on marketing over the Internet. The poor thing is always trying to bring her business up to date. But how could she, really, with wares so odd and odiferous (stinky)? Not many people realize how off-putting smelly books are. Most of us long to spray them with a good disinfectant (and I know my disinfectants). Thankfully, most university professors fail to care about such inconveniences, and they frequently show up at the shop despite all of that.

So the twins's lives weren't exactly perfect. They had to do chores, help out, and even endure being ignored or yelled at by snooty neighbors. And now with school starting in September, Uncle Auggie had said to them, "We'll expect you to make the grade."

Linus worried about that because he'd never tested well. You see, the children's parents had never so much as looked at their report cards. But Ophelia whispered to her brother, "Don't worry, Linus, I'll help you through. You know I will."

As they dried the dishes in the kitchen, a crisp rapping vibrated the back door of the store downstairs. Linus rushed down to open the door, and there stood Madrigal Pierce, the headmistress of the Kingscross School for Young People, a rather genteel yet run-down boarding school (which used to be the Pierce family mansion, built in 1811) located on the other side of the Seven Hills bookshop.

I must tell you, the school thinks itself snootier and more well-heeled than reality suggests. Most of the students come from backgrounds where their parents must sacrifice greatly—or rack up debt if they enjoy eating out and going to Disney World—in order to send them there. But nobody seems to realize it because they make themselves so busy by overstuffing their lives back home. One exception is Clarice Yardly-Poutsmouth. Her parents are richer than everybody else put together, but she never tells a soul.

"I saw you children loitering at the park today," Ms. Pierce said, her thin lips turned down over a perfect chin.

Paris Park sits on the Bard River; it's across the street and up a block.

"Hello, Ms. Pierce," Ophelia said as she stepped forward. "How are you today?"

"How can I get my students to behave when you're running around like ruffians?"

"But it's summer, and I'd hardly call throwing a baseball—"

"Don't contradict me!"

"Would you like a cup of tea?" Ophelia redirected the conversation.

"Why yes, thank you."

Madrigal Pierce always came to criticize and ended up staying for tea. Ophelia just has that way about her, you see. The woman, who seems to be around fifty years of age, gathered her summer shawl around her shoulders and paraded on her high heels through the bookshop and up the stairs to the family's living room. She kicked off her shoes and curled them beneath her on the couch.

It would be easy to describe her as unattractive to suit her personality; but, like Mr. Birdwistell and his name, Madrigal Pierce's looks and demeanor constantly warred against each other. In other words, she'd been a looker in her youth, and she remained a looker in her middle age. But believe me, I know to stay away from her. That's my advice to you as well.

"What are you reading?" She drilled Ophelia with questions like this every time she came by.

"*The Hunchback of Notre-Dame.* I just started reading it a few minutes ago."

"Victor Hugo. Good." She patted her hair. "Ah, the horrible Quasimodo. How different life would be for him today."

Ophelia, however, wasn't so sure about that. She'd been made fun of all her life because she loved to read and was a good student. She hated to think how Quasimodo would fare with the students at her old school.

"And while we're at it, Ophelia, my darling, I want to tell you about one of our new students. His name is Walter, and he's here all the way from London. So I thought, what with you and Linus being deserted by—pardon me—living away from your parents, perhaps you might help him adjust, give him a few pointers. He's the only one, other than Clarice, who's here for the summer, and I really don't wish to be bothered with worrying about him all the time. Clarice, as you know, can take care of herself."

Oh my, could she!

She really must be worried about him if she's asking us for help, Ophelia surmised (guessing with some insight attached).

"Send him over, Ms. Pierce. We'll show him around and help him feel at home in Kingscross."

"And so you should if you are decent children—which, I must add, still remains to be seen."

They finished their tea, and then Madrigal took her leave with a forceful, "I have to get back to raising funds for the school!" She obviously tried to make it sound positive, but Ophelia could tell she was only giving herself a pep talk.

Ophelia settled in her room for the evening with her book and a plate of cookies that Ronda, the neighborhood hair stylist, had brought by earlier in the day. You will adore Ronda! She can guess any song in three notes during a rousing game of Name That Tune.

Linus threw himself on Ophelia's bed. "Reading tonight?"

"What else? What are you going to do?"

He sighed. "Design some stocks, I guess."

"How exciting." She offered him the plate.

He bit down into a cookie and instantly brightened up. Cookies do that to a person, even more so than a cake or pie or, heaven forbid, candy.

While they didn't possess the proverbial nasty relatives, horrible food to eat, rags to wear, mysterious housekeepers, or windswept moors (wide open plains that go on and on), the twins were overcome by something else. Boredom. The ultimate enemy of children everywhere, if what they mutter to themselves while drifting about the house is to be believed.

"I might ask Clarice if she wants to take a walk," Linus said while staring at Ophelia.

Already engrossed in her book, she waved him off.

But not even ten minutes later, she started. Take a walk with Clarice? She hurried over to the window overlooking the street and watched as Linus and Clarice disappeared into Paris Park.

At least they aren't holding hands, she thought.

Later that night, Linus sat in the attic lab with a large glass of milk and some cookies. Sitting just underneath the trefoil window (looks somewhat like a shamrock), the moon shone on his face as he thought about plans for the stocks and wished for an adventure. Clarice came to mind. He liked her, but she sure didn't say much!

He opened his notebook and began sketching, scribbling down dimensions and making notes of how much wood and other materials he'd need for the project.

This is just what I need to get through the next few uneventful days, he thought. His eyes drifted about the room until they landed on the shelf full of potions and powders. He pursed his lips. I wonder if any of this stuff is still good?

Never one to hesitate, Linus reached for the bottle of rainbow liquid and the glass container labeled One. When he opened it, he saw a bright red powder caked inside as if it hadn't been touched in years. As he set a beaker on the table, Linus wondered if he should add the liquid to the powder or the powder to the liquid. He figured one was as good as the other when a guy knew absolutely nothing about what he was doing.

Linus grabbed a nearby letter opener, dug out a pinch of the mysterious red stuff, and then dropped it in the beaker. Best not to use too much at first, he thought. He pictured a purple, red, and gold column of fire rising through the roof and making a thunderous cloud over Kingscross.

Let's hope these things have lost their potency.

He took a sip of milk, then reached for the bottle of rainbow solution.

Praying a short, fervent "Dear God, please don't let me blow up the house" sort of prayer, he poured one drop of solution onto the powder and waited.

Three seconds. Four. Nothing.

Oh well. He tried two more drops. Still nothing. Then four more drops.

Suddenly the table shook, a green mist collected in the belly of the beaker, and then it disappeared in a snap.

And so did the glass of milk!

Interesting. Linus clearly needed to find out more about the works of one Cato Grubbs, the mad scientist of Rickshaw Street!

three

Party Like It's 1399

Or Enough! Let's Get the Plot Rolling!

Had Linus realized that he'd have to wear a pair of colorful pantyhose to this party, he might have left the house for the evening under false pretenses. (In other words, he might have lied and said he had a more pressing engagement elsewhere. Please don't judge him too harshly. Pantyhose will make certain fellows cast their principles down the river, and there's not much one can do about it.)

Ophelia felt no better as she put on the most ridiculous hat she'd ever seen. She could have worn the typical coned-shape hat that one sees all the time in women's medieval garb (fashion). But oh no! Hers had to have two cones.

"I look like an upholstered bull, thanks to Uncle Auggie," Ophelia moaned.

Linus nodded.

"Where does he find this stuff?"

Linus shrugged and shook his head.

"Can you make it disappear like that glass of milk in the attic?" she asked with hope aglow in her eyes.

"I wouldn't even try."

"And you look like a fool, Linus."

He adjusted the sleeves of his jester's costume. "I'm supposed to."

"Oh." She gathered her skirts. "Well, it's still silly looking."

Tell me about it, Linus thought. The mental image of their parents roughing it in bug-infested tents and eating those same bugs offered him only a bit of satisfaction.

A few minutes later, Linus and Ophelia entered the bookshop carrying trays of unrecognizable hors d'oeuvres made by Ronda from next door. She supplemented her income from the beauty shop with the occasional catering job. Medieval fare. Linus didn't want to ask.

Ronda's dark hair now glistened from the heat of the kitchen. An aside note: I mentioned previously that Headmistress Pierce of the Kingscross School for Young People is a looker. Well, Ronda might just stop your heart with her mahogany hair and aquamarine eyes.

As Ronda swiped the sweat from her brow with her forearm, she said to her reluctant servers, "If any of them dare ask what you're serving, you tell them to look it up. Those professors deserve it!" She punctuated her joke with one robust, "Ha!" heard all the way down the steps.

Obeying Uncle Auggie's instructions to be circumspect (proper, polite, and somewhat dull, really), they circulated amid the guests and offered them the disgusting bits. (No offense, dear Ronda.)

Ophelia leaned close to her brother's ear as they picked up another set of trays holding equally disconcerting (confusing, perplexing) morsels of food. "Do you think we'll have to do stuff like this the whole time we live here?" she asked.

"Yep," he replied.

Gazing over the crowd, Ophelia appreciated the colorful display before her—and not just the costumes, but the people themselves. An odd lot for certain, they were mainly university professors she figured. But there were also a few local business owners and several musicians present.

Augustus Sandwich had played the violin in the Boston Philharmonic as a young man, and he made it a point to never let good friendships go. I suggest you do the same.

Ophelia enjoyed eavesdropping on adults' conversations with topics ranging anywhere from gardening to Plato's *Republic* (a book which Ophelia hates, by the way; and I agree—give me Aristotle any day of the week). She enjoyed seeing their flushed faces and sparkling eyes as well, and she took some comfort in the fact that several of their costumes looked even more ridiculous than hers. Linus felt the same way.

The party spilled out onto the backyard where torches blazed and people posed in the stocks for a souvenir photo. (Linus had done a wonderful job building them.) Aunt Portia always insisted on providing souvenir photos at her parties—much to everyone's open dismay and secret delight. The air burgeoned (was filled to bursting) with laughter and the smell of the kerosene torches. A breeze picked up and shook the brightly colored flags hanging from clotheslines strung between long poles jammed into the ground.

This sure beats having to live on Butterfly Island, Ophelia thought as she headed back toward the kitchen for a new tray filled with odd food. When she passed Mr. Birdwistell, she offered him the last hors d'oeuvre on her tray. But he simply turned his back on her and continued his discussion with another professor, this one dressed like a friar.

Ronda, however, was delighted to snap up the suspicious morsel as soon as Ophelia entered the kitchen. She popped it in her mouth, chewed quickly, and swallowed. "When will you let me get to those curls, Ophelia?" Ronda asked as she reached out and sectioned off a portion of Ophelia's dark hair with her fingers.

"I like my hair, Ronda."

"I do too. I just think we should have some fun with it."

"Really?" Ophelia was intrigued.

"Let's chat about it soon."

Linus entered the kitchen and set his empty tray on the table. "Ready for more."

Aunt Portia came through the door right behind him. She was dressed in a gown made of lime green gauze that fluttered in the breeze and a Juliet style cap with a trail of matching fabric. She sashayed (glided, walked smoothly) over to the tray-filled table and threaded her arm through Ronda's. "I went to that marketing class, and you'll never guess what I bought as a result!"

"I'm sure I can't," said Ronda.

"An LED message board! I can put funny sayings to go running across, tell people about sales and intriguing finds—right there in the front window of the store!"

"Well, let me have a look! I just arranged the dessert table, so I have a few free minutes." Ronda placed her hand over Portia's, and they disappeared down the steps and into the shop.

Ophelia shook her head. Old books and LED signs. Some things just didn't seem to mix. But if anybody could make it work, it was Aunt Portia.

Did I hear someone say dessert table? thought Linus.

four

A Third Wheel Is Important
if You're Riding a Tricycle

Or Welcoming the Character That Rounds Things Out

Quiet people get thorny about other people's assumptions that they'd rather be left alone. Linus, although the quiet one of the twins, prefers company. While Ophelia, chatty and bossy as she is, could be alone all day long if she found the book engaging enough. Let's just say that fictional characters were every bit as real to Ophelia as flesh and blood people and, as she put it, "A whole lot more predictable."

Once they'd finished their serving duties, Aunt Portia released them back upstairs to their rooms and asked them to straighten things a bit, thanks.

Both twins got busy tossing books around their room. Ophelia shelved titles like *Jane Eyre*, *Fahrenheit 451*, or *The Federalist Papers*, while Linus's books were about ancient building techniques, the mystery of the pyramids, aerodynamics, and how to make a combustible engine from the contents of your average junk drawer. (I fancied he would build a plane someday, just to see if he could.)

Their bedroom walls were covered in different shades of blue, which they both loved. Ophelia was drawn to deep midnight blues and indigos, while Linus preferred sky blue and ... well, sky blue. While Ophelia pinned up posters of long-dead movie stars and baby animals, Linus tacked up nothing. Instead, he used his walls to figure out equations and draw his own pictures. He really is quite the artist. And Ophelia fancies herself someday making yard sculptures out of bits of junk. But for now, a pile of junk sits in one corner of her room, much to the dismay of Aunt Portia who doesn't understand the idiosyncrasies (quirks) of artistic creativity, probably owing to the fact that she cannot draw the simplest stick figure.

Linus looked at his clock. It was now 10:30 p.m. and the party downstairs had finally wound down. Maybe a snack would be a good idea. After all, he had to frequently nourish that tall body of his. As he stepped out into the hallway, just at the top of the steps, he heard a rustle from the bathroom. More than a rustle, really. Perhaps one could describe it as the whisper of wood grating on wood.

He peered into the room just as a square of paneling near the toilet was pushed out of the way, and a head of gleaming brown hair emerged, followed by a long, muscular neck and broad shoulders swaddled in light blue pajamas. At that moment the head looked up to reveal a florid (red) face with large green-blue eyes that grew even larger at the sight of Linus.

Linus tilted his head.

"Oh!" the boy said. "Sorry."

Warm voice, British accent ... this must be Walter, the new student at The Kingscross School that Ophelia had mentioned earlier.

"No problem."

"I found this secret passage. Where am I?" He crawled completely out of the opening now, his movements very graceful and athletic — almost like a big cat.

"Next door. Bookshop." Linus eyed the boy's arms, which were twice as big as his own. Those could come in handy for some heavy lifting in the future.

Walter stood up and dusted himself off before offering Linus his hand, "Well. So here I am. Walter Liddel."

Linus quickly sized him up and had to admit that Walter could probably take him (beat him in a fight).

"Linus Easterday."

"Pleasure."

"How old are you?"

"Fourteen."

Wow. How big will he be when he fills out? Linus thought. Out loud he said, "Same."

"Good heavens, how tall do you think you'll be when you stop growing?"

Linus shook his head with a shrug. "Want something to eat?"

Walter screwed up his face. "I can't tell you how much. The food over there ..." he tilted his head in the direction of the school and shuddered.

Linus could only imagine.

"And there's never enough of it either. You know Clarice? She eats enough to feed two grown men!"

Linus tucked that away for future reference. If he ever took her out to dinner, it would have to be someplace offering a two-for-one special.

The boys wandered into the kitchen and began eating party leftovers. Walter knew what some of them were, what with his hailing from England. There were quail eggs and beef wellington. (Although why a dish from the 1800s was included in a medieval feast, I could not say. I suppose Augustus failed to hit all of the targets with that party.) There were also sausages, which both lads dipped right into the mustard jar. And to wash it all down, they drank soda (or pop, as some folks call it)—glasses and glasses of soda. In this case, they drank watermelon and green apple flavors. I don't wish to know what's in those sodas. It's most likely radioactive.

Now what just happened here, as far as plotting goes, is that Linus received a compatriot, someone to rely on in a very different way than he can rely on his sister. Not that he loves her any less, but the two of them have so little in common. Plus, Linus feels more protective of his sibling than he does of some new guy from a different country.

Walter also rounds out the group rather nicely, as neither twin is particularly physical in nature. Ophelia succumbs to nausea on spinning apparatuses and, due to an overdeveloped sense of competition, has avoided team sports because of the ugliness that comes out in her. Meanwhile, Linus despises heights; and while his fine motor skills are keen (I would bet all of my cleaning supplies that the boy could paint the Last Supper on the head of a pin), he can barely walk down a set of steps without a bit of a stumble. That he didn't tip a single tray of quail eggs onto a guest that night was nothing short of miraculous.

So you can see how Walter, with his physical prowess, strength, and a certain indefinable charm, rounds out this trio quite well. When you find yourself in an adventure, try to bring along a person of charm—not to mention downright sparkling good looks and compelling personality—to serve as a decoy. He'll get you into the places you need to go but would otherwise be shut out due to your lack of the gift of gab.

I was busy those days or, rest assured, I would have volunteered myself.

fiße

Sometimes Unexpected Guests Prove to Have Arrived at Precisely the Right Time

While Linus was busy meeting Walter, Ophelia had retreated to the attic space with two books in hand. At any given time, Ophelia could be in the midst of reading several books. However, since she'd just finished *The Good Earth*, she was now involved in only two: her grandmother's Bible, which she was reading for the third time, and *The Hunchback of Notre-Dame*.

Her eyes now flicked back and forth from the book of Esther to the current conditions of Quasimodo. And while her grandmother had underlined a verse about loving your enemies, Ophelia felt more like throttling someone! Anyone in that Parisian mob would do.

Oh, that poor hunchback! Ophelia loved the downtrodden, the oppressed, and the underdog (a person not accepted by the "in" crowd or, as in a contest, the one most likely to lose; also, the least likely to be picked for anyone's team on the playground. Yet, who'd want to be picked by those horrible, insensitive, unfair, and stupid people anyway?). Quasimodo—his name meaning "part man" or "semi-human"—wanted what we all do: to love and to be loved in return. Unfortunately, when you live in a cathedral and most of your conversations are with the same one or two people, the chance of that happening is severely diminished.

In addition, if your spine is curled at the top like a shepherd's crook, while bristly patches of red hair sprout from your oversized head, a giant wart covers one of your eyes, and some unknown manner of growth protrudes from your forehead ... well, then you should probably cast aside any notion of finding that special someone to take you out to a cozy candlelit dinner at your favorite French restaurant. And being deaf, due to your job as a bell ringer in the cathedral's tower, affords no great help to the matter. But at least you can speak. You still have that going for you, at any rate (although what you might have to say, having lived in a cathedral your entire life, I cannot begin to guess). Such were the circumstances of Quasimodo.

Now, loving other people wasn't hard for Quasimodo. It was the receiving love part that never seemed to work in his favor. He loved his caretaker, Deacon Frollo, the priest who found him on the steps of the Notre-Dame Cathedral in Paris, took him in, raised him, taught him, and provided a place of sanctuary. And in some ways, Frollo loved him too. But it was a harsh love, a demanding kind of affection through which Quasimodo realized that most of life's offerings come at a price. We all have to realize that some-day—and the sooner the better, I say. Why, consider some of those English professors I mentioned earlier, who take for granted all of my support and encouragement. They shall be sorry one day when I can take it no more.

But most importantly, at least for our story, Quasimodo loved the graceful Esmeralda, a beautiful Gypsy girl with long, dark, lustrous, curly hair and tiny feet. She danced in the cathedral square and performed tricks with her little goat, Djali (pronounced "Jolly"). Crowds gathered around her, mesmerized by her beauty and the magnetism of her personality. In other words, she knew how to put on a good show. But how could a girl like Esmeralda ever come to love a man like Quasimodo, even though he had the strength of ten men?

Impossible.

But permit me to tell you something: There are many kinds of love in the world, so if we don't find ourselves possessing one variety, plenty more exist in which to invest.

You might think Quasimodo would have a difficult time find-ing any kind of love, what with the wart and all. But consider this, if someone cannot look beyond a giant wart, bristly hair, a hunched back, and spindly legs (or a large nose, eyes that protrude a bit too far, crooked teeth, or an addicted parent), then perhaps the love that person offers to the world is not true love at all.

That evening in the attic, Ophelia wondered if she would have treated Quasimodo any differently on that January day when he wandered out of Notre-Dame. Through no fault of his own, Quasimodo was unanimously elected as Pope of Fools on Epiphany, or the Feast of Fools, which was a holiday in Paris during the Middle Ages when her citizens, particularly the students, felt a little more license (in this case, freedom) to unveil, shall we say, all of their personality.

Ophelia, despite her preoccupation with whatever book she is reading, owned a soft heart. After the anger subsided, she felt sorrow for Quasimodo as she lay there on the blue sofa. At the insistence of Frollo, his master and father figure who was also in love (to the point of obsession) with the Gypsy girl Esmeralda, Quasimodo tried to kidnap her. Unfortunately, luck was not on his side—left, right, front, or back—and he was arrested and thrown into jail. Meanwhile, Frollo escaped into the night with a swirl of his black cape. Obviously, he enjoyed a good deal more luck than his charge did.

And luck may not have been in play so much as Frollo's obsession with alchemy and magic. Could that have given him the confidence he needed to escape? It certainly didn't make him love Quasimodo more.

So the officials of Paris pushed Quasimodo into the stocks the next day.

Just in case you may not be familiar with them, stocks are a wooden device that was used to trap a person by the hands and neck—feet, too, if he were unlucky enough—while the public was invited, even encouraged, to ridicule the prisoner. But the real ones weren't created for taking souvenir pictures at a party in some college town. These bit the wrists and squeezed the neck with their wooden jaws if you were large enough, and Quasimodo was most definitely large enough. How far down the Pope of Fools had fallen—paraded around the city one day, displayed as a criminal with rotten produce and street garbage hurled at his face the next.

Ophelia's heart broke again for the character. If she'd been there, she would have gotten him out of those stocks—or at the very least brought him some water.

Oh, that poor young man!

Before she lifted the book back into her field of vision, something else made its way there. Two things, actually: a three-inch high carving atop a book on the worktable under the window. She set her book on the floor, just inside the painted circle, and got up to take a closer look. She picked up the figurine and studied it. A little dove rested on the stump of a tree, looking as if it were about to take flight.

The book beneath it proved most interesting. It was called, *It's All Reality: Traveling Through "Imaginary" Realms in Five Easy Steps.* Ophelia opened the volume, hardly old, its glossy cover sporting the picture of a man, thumbs up, amid characters Ophelia recognized right away. The Ghost of Christmas Present with a candelabra wreath atop his giant head, Miss Havisham in her moth-eaten bridal gown, Hamlet (if the doublet and the wild look in the man's eyes was any clue), Natty Bumppo, and Hester Prynne (she was easy to recognize what with wearing that glowing scarlet A on her dress).

This looks like a photograph, Ophelia thought, realizing she was quite possibly holding the strangest book she'd ever seen. She positively knew it hadn't been there when she'd reclined on the sofa an hour earlier. Had she dozed off and not realized it? Who dropped it off? Linus? Had he found it in the bookshop? Surely she would have heard him come into the attic.

She shivered. *I don't like this.*

Wary, Ophelia brought the book back to the couch and opened it on her lap. She felt tired. Maybe she should start on it in the morning. The attic was beginning to make her skin crawl (or "creep her out," as she so eloquently described). She checked her watch— 11:10 p.m. Ophelia loved elevens, and 11:11 was her favorite time of the day and night, so she watched the display on her watch until it switched.

At 11:11 on the dot, the room began vibrating, the tubes and beakers clinked against each other, the fringe on the couch pillows jiggled side by side. Even the milk in her glass broadcast itself from center to edge in concentric circles (one inside the other like rings inside a tree). Ophelia held on to the arm of the sofa and raised her feet up off the floor.

An earthquake? In Kingscross?

Her eyes became the size of large gumballs as she looked down and watched the circle on the floor begin to glow, blue at first, then green, then yellow, orange, red, pink, and on into violet. Suddenly, white sparks (imagine sparklers) shot up from the floor as if someone had placed nozzles all around the circle. They hissed and popped and made the William Tell Overture jump into Ophelia's brain. She wanted to run, but she felt as if an unseen hand pressed her to the couch cushion.

And all was still.

Smoke, faint and smelling more like baby powder than flame, fogged the room. And then with a swirling snap, it all disintegrated.

Ophelia rubbed her eyes and looked inside the painted circle on the floor.

What?

She rubbed her eyes again. I must be seeing things!

A large figure sat hunched over in the middle of the circle. He raised his head, took one look at Ophelia with his good eye and then scanned the room around him. He inhaled a shaky breath and fainted, falling forward with a thud.

six

Worlds Collide and the Instructions Aren't as Helpful as One Should Expect

Generally speaking, Ophelia is no dolt. She knew right away who was passed out inside the circle. Who else could be cursed with a wart so big that it covered one eye? After all, we have surgeons for that sort of thing nowadays.

"Quasimodo!" She dropped to her knees beside the huddled mass that, not to sound cruel, smelled like a dumpster in August.

I don't understand, she thought. *How did he get here?*

The book! She grabbed the *Imaginary Realms* book from where it was lying open on the couch, and ran her finger down the table of contents.

INTRODUCTION

That's the chapter she wanted! She quickly turned to page seventy-seven. "Whoa!"

Her eyes settled on a diagram of a circle in the book, similar to the one painted near her feet. The measurements listed in the text were very peculiar. The circle had to be exactly five feet, eleven-and-seven-eighths inches in diameter. The border around the circle was to be two-and-five-sixths inches wide and painted off-white, "Sherwin Williams eggshell, preferably" was hand-written in the book.

> Travel from imaginary realms must take place on
> the eleventh day of the month at 11:11 p.m. And
> if a gibbous moon is shining (when the moon is
> neither full nor a crescent, but a bulgy phase in
> between), then so much the better. There must
> be a westward facing window in the room, and if
> it's raining or the cloud cover is especially thick,
> it might not work. But then again, it might.
> Who's to say?

"Umm ... you?" Who wrote this thing? She turned back to the title page. The author was a Mr. C. G. Grubbs. Cato! The mad scientist! How many other people had gotten their hands on this little piece of intriguing instruction? If it were to fall into the wrong hands, Ophelia figured, the book could do great damage. Just imagine bringing Julius Caesar to present day. What would that do to the world?

She read on, keeping one eye on the page and the other on Quasimodo who was still passed out in a heap but breathing evenly.

> Place your chosen book of literature inside the
> circle. If the name of the character you wish
> to call forth isn't in the title, circle it at first
> reference

That makes sense, she thought, recalling the title of her own book, *The Hunchback of Notre-Dame.*

Whatever you do, don't get inside the circle
unless you wish to be whisked off into the world
of the book. If you do wish for that, then by all
means get in. But be warned: most folks return as
quite different people.

Ophelia could think of a lot of places she'd rather travel to than
fourteenth-century Paris. As she thought about the many books
she loves to read, she realized they all play out in rather dreary
settings, and the main characters always face particularly sad challenges. While she loved reading about them within the book, she
certainly wouldn't want to be caught in the middle of all of that
doom and gloom. Come to think of it, she had been feeling a little
depressed of late.

Maybe I'd better read something more fun, she thought. *Something more age appropriate and with more fantastical elements—
or at the very least, devoted canines.*

Quasimodo's arm muscle jerked a bit and quickly brought Ophelia back to the present.

Hurry up, she thought, though it was *she* who had to hurry up
reading.

Do realize that your life will now be fraught with
varying challenges, depending on the character.
Some will be more difficult than others, so
choose wisely because you'll have this person
with you for a while.

In the event that you don't get the character
returned to the circle in time, he or she will
expire painfully and with great pop and sizzle
and acidic vapor — much like the Wicked Witch
of the West (although, unless your chosen
character is that woman, he or she most likely
won't screech, 'I'm melting! I'm melting!' as

it happens). Some characters, of course, might deserve that type of an end. But I assure you, it takes weeks for the fumes to clear, and your activities may become known to others — so be prudent.

Under no circumstances can the character return before the appointed time, so you'll just have to figure it out. You brought the person here; you have nobody to blame but yourself.

On the third day, just sixty hours after arrival, departure is scheduled for 11:11 a.m. — and only then. Remember, "a.m." means morning, not nighttime. Count on it. Otherwise, the result, as I've already tried to tell you, isn't pretty. Good luck!

Ophelia set down the book. Three days. Three days with Quasimodo, a medieval, Parisian hunchback recluse, right here in Kingscross, right here in this house, right here in the enchanted circle.

"What happened to my plate of cookies?" Ophelia mused aloud. It was nowhere that she could see.

She went to find Linus.

seven

Mystery Loves Company

Linus figured that with the unexpected arrival of Walter, he was in possession of a certain element of surprise over his sister. Was he ever wrong about that!

Ophelia began to explain things as the three of them made their way to the attic. "You'll never believe this." Then she stopped and pointed to Walter. "I don't know who you are, but I'm going to have to trust you because there's no time to interview you." Apparently, she hadn't yet noticed the comeliness (handsomeness) of her brother's new friend. Or so she claims.

"You can trust him." Linus assured his sister as he followed her up the narrow staircase, Walter close behind. "He's that British guy."

"No need to worry," Walter said. "I've seen more than a few odd things in my life."

"Okay. Just nobody talk, all right? I don't know what he'll do."

"Who's he?" asked Linus.

"Quasimodo, the hunchback of Notre-Dame!"

Both boys stopped.

Walter shook his head and acted like he was unstopping his ears. "Did you say what I think you just said?"

"She did," said Linus, trying to keep calm. He'd never known his sister to be hysterical, fantastical, or delusional. "Maybe it's a figment of your imagination."

"It is not, Linus. You know me better than that. It's something Cato Grubbs designed."

Walter blew out a huge puff of air and rubbed his hands together. "Well, the only way to find out is to see it for ourselves. Is he safe?"

"Passed out cold right now," said Ophelia.

"There must be a good explanation for this," said Linus.

But when the boys took one look at Quasimodo, Linus drew in his breath sharply and Walter whispered, "This isn't possible."

"I assure you it is," Ophelia whispered back.

"We should awaken him gently." Walter squatted next to Quasimodo.

Linus joined him, nodding.

Ophelia crossed her arms. "Go ahead. I'd rather him rear up against you two than me."

Linus reached out and touched the wart.

"Linus!" Ophelia hissed.

Walter took a deep breath. "Right then. Let's give this a go." He rubbed a light, small circle on Quasimodo's back, just below the hump. "Quasimodo," he said softly. Then he repeated the name, slightly louder this time.

The hunchback shifted and moaned, the sound barely audible. He opened his eye. It widened. Then he hollered—sort of a grunt, really, but with a bit more heft or strength. He sat up, immediately cowered, and raised his arms to cover his massive head.

"He's frightened of us," Walter said.

"He's been living in a cathedral all of his life," Ophelia told the boys.

She stepped forward and leaned down next to Quasimodo. Sitting back on her heels, she slowly extended a hand toward him before gently placing it on Quasimodo's forearm. "Bonjour," she said quietly.

A look of confusion crossed his face.

"Hello," Ophelia tried again.

He nodded.

She turned to Linus. "I wonder why he didn't understand French?"

"Maybe because the book is written in English?"

"Ahh. Right." She turned back. "I'm Ophelia."

He shook his head.

Ophelia shook hers. "That's right! He's deaf from all of that bell ringing. I should have remembered that."

"Madge has hearing aids," Walter offered.

"Madge?" Ophelia asked.

"Ms. Pierce."

Ophelia laughed. "Can you borrow a set?"

"Please. I'm a street rat from London." He disappeared through the attic doorway.

"He might be hungry," Linus said. Linus thought good food cured just about everything. Then he screwed up his face. "He smells terrible."

"If my guess is right and he came from the point in the book where I was last reading, then he was just in the stocks," Ophelia explained.

She made an eating sign, bringing her hand up to her mouth and pretending to bite something.

Quasimodo nodded and said, "Yes, I'm hungry."

The twins jumped at the sound of his voice.

"Good, he can speak!"

"I'll get food," Linus said, leaving Ophelia alone with the hunchback of Notre-Dame.

eight

When in Doubt, Get Something to Eat

ow don't start thinking that just because someone has scolio-
sis (curvature of the spine), he is different in every other way
as well. It would be easy to commit such a crime against another
human being. People do it all the time. It makes them feel more
important. However, those kinds of gross conclusions (other than
the ones concerning the English professors in my department, of
course) simply aren't true and can lead to a lifetime of ignorance.
The boys did no such thing.

Linus and Walter (who got those hearing aids so quickly that
one had to wonder if his street rat career included pickpocketing)
skillfully raided the refrigerator as though they were getting an
armful of snacks for themselves.

Upstairs, Quasimodo took one look at Ophelia in her medieval
costume and with her long, curly dark hair, and he figured she had
to be related to Esmeralda. Clearly she wasn't so different from
him. Ophelia ventured to take hold of Quasimodo's hand, and, to
her surprise, he allowed it. Not knowing what else to do, she simply sat with him and tried smiling every so often, which proved
to be rather difficult. It broke her heart to think so, but he was the
ugliest human being she'd ever seen. Not a single resting point
could be found on his face, that normal spot on which you might
cast your eyes to take a breather from all the other deformities. Oh
no. Nothing of the sort. The only place that looked anything like
it should was his left earlobe, and who wants to look at that while
you're speaking to someone?

His breathing softened and his muscles gradually relaxed as Ophelia lightly patted his hand, which, I might point out, was roughly four times the size of hers. She remembered reading that he was only about nineteen years old, not so much older than her own little group. But he looked so very, very old—at least forty years. So old, one might say, as to be of little use to society because who can walk around in such a decrepit state?

When the boys returned to the attic, both Ophelia and Quasimodo hungrily eyed the tray heaped with food. Peanut butter, jelly, bread, corn chips, jelly donuts, chocolate covered donuts, bananas, and sitting on top for good measure, a tomato. That last one was Walter's idea. Something needed to balance out all of that sugar, for heaven's sake.

Linus rolled his eyes at that.

I'm sure you can guess that the tomato was the only thing that remained on that tray when all was said and done.

Ophelia spread some peanut butter and raspberry jelly on a piece of bread. She split it in half, took a bite of hers, and then offered the other half to Quasimodo.

He eyed it with suspicion.

"Eat," she said. "Good."

He understood, took the sandwich, and bit down.

A look of amazement flashed across his face.

"You like it?"

Ophelia overly enunciated (pronounced) her words so he could read her lips.

"Yes."

So let us give Quasimodo his fair share of credit here. His voice, while somewhat husky from lack of use, sounded just fine. He spoke clearly, and his tones were friendly and without suspicion. If somebody were to assign them a color, one might say they were an orangey-gold.

They soon finished off the tray of food together—the boys helped.And with each new food item, Ophelia employed the same method. Seeing as it worked so well with the food, she tried the same thing with the hearing aids. Putting one in her ear and the other in Quasimodo's, she leaned over and asked, "Are you Quasimodo? The bell ringer of Notre-Dame?"

His good eye widened and he nodded his head. Then he patted his ear and flinched. Touched the hearing aid more carefully this time, he said, "Yes, I am. I heard you! I just heard every word you said!"

An expression of amazed joy spread over his face, and suddenly he didn't seem so horrific at all!

Quick introductions were made, and then Ophelia asked if they could call him "Quasi." He said yes. Then she tried her best to explain what had happened to him—minus the fact that he wasn't actually real, not in the sense of being born here on planet Earth, to physical parents in a physical place during a definite time period. And never mind the fact that she could touch him just as she could touch you or me. (You, preferably. You never know where people's hands have been.)

This took quite awhile, and when she showed Quasi her copy of *The Hunchback of Notre-Dame*, he almost jumped off the floor. "This is ... about me?"

"Yes."

He flipped it over, examining its spine. "It's so small. And this cover –"

"Paperback," she said. "They're everywhere these days."

"Not just in churches and libraries?"

"No. And most people can read now. You can read, right?"

"Yes. Frollo taught me." His eyes clouded.

"Do you want to talk about it, mate?" asked Walter, a jelly donut halfway to his mouth.

"No."

Linus didn't blame him.

"We'll talk about Frollo later. His alchemy is intriguing, to say the least," said Ophelia. "He's not very nice, is he?"

"I'd rather not say," said Quasi.

"Are you tired?" Ophelia asked. "That was quite a journey, I'm guessing."

He nodded his heavy head, reminding Ophelia of a horse. "Too much for one day. I start out in prison and end up five hundred and thirty years in the future with no idea about what comes next." He paused. "Do they hang people here?"

"No. You'll be all right," said Ophelia.

"That's a relief."

"What did it feel like?" asked Walter. "The trip here?"

Good question, thought Linus.

Quasimodo looked toward the ceiling, thinking. "Do you ever feel like you're falling right before you go to sleep?"

"Yes!" Ophelia said.

"It felt like that—only you're falling up, not down."

"Awful?" asked Linus.

"Not terrible. But I am tired."

"A good night's sleep will help, to be sure," Ophelia said as she patted his arm and stood up. "We'll get you set up."

As quietly as they could, the boys brought up an extra mattress from under Linus's bed, while Ophelia found some sheets, a pillow, and her favorite quilt.

Fascinated, Quasimodo watched as they made up his bed. "Does everyone sleep like kings?"

"I guess so," said Ophelia.

By now the boys had gone back to their own rooms, so once she'd tucked in Quasimodo and made sure he was sleeping, Ophelia settled herself onto the blue sofa and checked her watch.

Six a.m.

Fifty-three hours left. What on earth were they going to do with him until then?

nine

Who Knew the Bathroom Was Such an Amazing Place?

If you ever end up with a medieval hunchback in your attic, my advice is to read this chapter very carefully and take note.

"It wouldn't be right not to show him around," Walter said the next morning. "If what you say is true, and he's basically been in captivity all of his life, then it's up to us to show him a good time."

It was 10 a.m., and the little group was now sitting in Paris Park while Quasimodo napped. They forsook the bandstand and the playground equipment, choosing to sit in the grass by the new skateboard park instead. Nobody was using it just then, but Linus could imagine them scooping out the bowl with their boards. People walked their dogs and cut across the green from one side of the square to the other. The Bard River flowed by on the north end, much as it always does. Not much to report really, other than Clarice Yardly-Poutsmouth was hitting a tennis ball against the backboard by the courts, while Linus thought about how cute she looked.

Ho hum. I would like to make this part extremely interesting, but it simply is not. I could add all variety of activity—a large birthday party with laughing children, a clown, and a pony; a work crew building a gazebo; an old woman pounding a would-be thief with a giant purple handbag; aliens landing among the trees; or even particularly uncoordinated people walking and chewing gum at the same time. However, that would be, simply put, false information.

"Quasi will be a little conspicuous out here, don't you think?"

Ophelia asked, picking a stem of grass and splitting it down the middle.

"Of course," said Walter. "We'll just have to disguise him."

"As what?" Ophelia said. "An oversized beggar woman? Not in this day and age. And besides, where would we take him?"

Linus pointed to the church across the way, All Souls Episcopal Church. "He might feel more at home there."

Ophelia couldn't help herself. She was so excited she kissed Linus on the cheek. "Linus, you're a genius! It's perfect."

Linus wiped his cheek and glared at Walter when he smiled. "We still have to get him over there," Linus said quickly, trying to turn the attention off himself.

"Maybe we can sneak him over there after dark." Walter said, and crossed his legs in front of him.

As Ophelia describes it (with a crimson blush), this is the point when she began to notice Walter's good looks, and she could hardly believe he was their age. What did they feed people in England anyway?

"I know," said Walter, "I'll go over there today and talk to the rector."

"No!" Ophelia and Linus said together.

He waved the word away. "I'm not going to tell him what we're actually planning. Do you think I'm daft? As far as he's concerned, we're junior astronomers. And besides that, I'm English. We're the original Episcopalians ... Anglicans, actually. But anyhow, that should go a long way."

"That's brilliant!" cried Ophelia. Her imagination began spinning a mental image of a rather massive king named Henry the Eighth who created the Anglican Church (or Church of England) because he disagreed with the Roman Catholic Church. She sure wouldn't want to bring him through the circle.

Linus nodded. "Let's go check on Quasi."

"I like Quasi a lot," Ophelia said. "He's nice."

"And he looks like he could lift a cow." Walter got to his feet. "I'd wager he would make mincemeat of all the lads at the gym."

Great, thought Linus, as he caught Ophelia surreptitiously (secretly) eyeing Walter's muscles. Another weightlifter.

Ophelia was prone (inclined, tended) to develop crushes on the more athletic boys. Unfortunately for her, or perhaps fortunately, boys like that usually shunned bookworms like Ophelia. More "important" matters typically demanded their time, such as looking at themselves in the mirror, buying supplements at the mall, or just about anything else that would be considered self-consumed and shallow, the blighters (scoundrels, rascals)! Ophelia was destined to be disappointed if she failed to reconsider her preferences.

The three hurried home and entered the attic, only to find Quasimodo sitting on his mattress reading *The Hunchback of Notre-Dame*. When he saw them come into the room, he flung it down, eyes wide.

"It's all right." Ophelia sat down next to him. "You can read it."

"It's very bleak at the beginning. That poor playwright. You'd think people would be more polite."

"You'd think," agreed Linus who could remember his first role in a play. He'd been the Bethlehem Star. Not one line. And not one compliment afterward either. Didn't the audience realize how hard it was to stand still for that long?

"Oh, people are generally rude all around," Walter said as he picked up the little wooden carving of the dove that was still sitting where Ophelia had left it the night before.

"Any other observations about the book?" Ophelia asked Quasi.

"He describes my stepfather perfectly."

"Oh him!" said Ophelia. "He needs to get a job."

"Huh?" Quasi said.

"That's just something we say when people keep asking their relatives for money."

"Oh. Well, you're right," he sighed. "No matter what I do, Frollo never—"

"Don't think about him." Ophelia stood up. "He's never going to fully approve of you. So don't even try to make that happen. Believe me, I know what I'm talking about."

Quasimodo looked down, hiding his sadness. Of course, he wasn't aware of the Drs. Easterday.

Walter, however, jumped on her words. "You're never going to get approval from whom, exactly?"

51

"Our parents," said Ophelia, and then she briefly explained the situation.

"Five years?" said Walter, knowing his mum wouldn't leave him for that long. Not in a hundred million years.

Ophelia offered her hand to Quasi. "Now, we probably should sneak you downstairs to the bathroom. I'm sure you'll want to clean up a bit."

"Why?" He took her hand and let her believe she was pulling him to his feet.

"You're not in medieval France anymore, Quasi. People take baths here. A lot."

"Oh." Worry creased his brow. "Medieval?" he asked.

"The historical time period from which you came. We name everything nowadays. You've entered the post-modern era."

He shrugged. "All right."

"Now, you'll have to be quiet. Aunt Portia and Uncle Auggie can't know you're here, or they'll never let us up here again. Not to mention the fact that they're too old to handle anything this crazy."

Fourteen-year-olds know everything, you know.

"I'm actually quite light on my feet." He blushed.

Pride did not motivate his statement. In fact, it was quite the understatement when you consider the fact that Quasimodo could climb all around the Notre-Dame Cathedral, swinging from beams and gargoyles and windowsills. Rock climbers could learn a thing or two from this young man. Gymnasts as well. Despite Quasi's deformities, a monkey would have nothing on him up there. So he most certainly could sneak down a set of stairs and into the bathroom. People have been trying to get to the bathroom quietly since there's been indoor plumbing. Why would Quasimodo be any different?

Well, you can imagine what someone from medieval times thought about a flushing toilet—about going into the toilet in general. Oh, the things we take for granted, my dears! But he soon caught on to the whole "running water" arrangement we have now (and thank goodness, I say!). In fact, he had a grand time turning the faucets on and off. With each on and off, he'd suck in his breath with glee. He almost shouted too, but then he remembered he was supposed to be a secret to the rest of the world. Quasimodo normally tried to be accommodating (go along with someone else's plan).

While the boys helped him into the tub—the shower was just too disconcerting (mildly disturbing) for someone who took a bath probably once a year—Ophelia went to the costume room to find something suitable for Quasimodo to wear. If you assumed his clothing was a wreck, smelly and greasy and raggedy, then you assumed correctly. Ophelia could no more imagine putting those dirty rags back on a clean body than she could putting a freshly grilled steak into that morning's cereal bowl. (I must add that I'm very glad I did not witness this infested garb [clothing] myself! Some things one never gets over.)

Hearing some thumps, bumps, and a loud "Shhhh!" or two, she imagined Quasi's displeasure at the idea of a bath—a person does have limits. Sliding the hangers across the pole, the array of costumes took her swiftly through the ages from caveman to Sumerian, through Greeks and Romans, the Dark Ages, the Middle Ages, the Renaissance, and oh bother! Uncle Augustus should have opened a costume shop!

Finally, she settled upon a pirate costume with brown breeches (knee pants), a leather vest, and a white shirt with a wide collar. Even better, the outfit would feel more familiar to him than cargo shorts and a band T-shirt.

Perfect.

She grabbed the costume, hanger and all, and slipped it through to the boys in the bathroom. As she did so, she heard Walter say, "You have to wash your hair, Quasi. It looks like porcupine quills there's so much dirt in there."

"What's a 'porcupine'?"

Ophelia stifled a giggle as she turned away.

She hurried back to the attic to make the bed and tidy the place a bit, and there on the worktable sat an empty milk glass and her plate of now nonexistent cookies. Nothing surprised her anymore. She gathered up the empty dishes just as Cato Grubbs' instruction book began to rumble and the pages began to flip. They stopped at page thirty-three, and the words in bold print caught Ophelia's attention:

If you haven't finished reading the novel by 11:11 a.m., the summoned character's plight will be the same — whether he or she is inside the circle or not.

Ophelia sucked in her breath. "Oh no! Part of this is up to me?"

She deposited the dirty dishes in the kitchen sink, washed them as quickly as she could (while still meeting Uncle Auggie's high standards), and rushed back up to her room.

She laid down on her bed, scooped up the copy of *The Hunchback of Notre-Dame*, and settled back in for the read. It was now 2 p.m.; that meant there were forty-five hours left, and she still had hundreds of pages left to read.

After Quasimodo asked for a carving knife and a block of wood, Linus walked two blocks down Rickshaw Street to Broderick's Hobby Shop and purchased the required materials. Meanwhile, Walter was visiting the rector of All Souls, no doubt charming Father Wellborne with a story about his love for astronomy and the opportunity to look at Jupiter from the vantage point of the church's bell tower later that night—all while having a lovely pot of tea.

"Finally!Someone who knows how to make a decent cup!" Walter reported later when they reconvened (gathered together again) in the attic. "At 10 p.m. we can head to the top of the tower."

Quasimodo's eyes gleamed. "What about the bells? Will I get to ring them?"

"The church bells are automated now," Linus said.

When Ophelia explained to Quasi that this basically meant the bells rang themselves, he looked as if he was going to cry.

"But it will be good to at least be up there with them, right?" she said, placing that calming hand on his arm once again.

He nodded and continued carving what looked like a dancing woman.

Oh great, thought Ophelia, *that nitwit Esmeralda*.

Just then a raindrop hit the trefoil window.

And another. And then another.

None of them knew it at the time, but the real trouble was about to begin. And soon enough, trying to contain and entertain the hunchback of Notre-Dame would be the least of their worries.

ten

If Only Noah Had Come Through the Enchanted Circle

*A*t the end of the last chapter, I added some tension to the story. If things had continued along in the same vein, then you might have set down the book and hopped onto a computer somewhere. And we all know that some shortsighted knuckle-heads designed those devices to turn people's brains to porridge (hot breakfast cereal, like oatmeal)—especially children's. The powers that be—and nobody knows who they really are—want to make sure the next generation turns into a flock of mindless sheep. Corporations and conglomerates (a grouping of corporations) are able to get more of your money that way.

You may be wondering what harm a few raindrops can cause. Well, a few raindrops do little but remind one of the corny rhyming song, "Rain, rain, go away, come again another day." But when rain-drops continue to fall and collect upon themselves, it becomes an entirely different matter. Ask Noah. He could tell you more about it than I could while sitting here behind my old typewriter in my little closet in the English department.

Ophelia spent the afternoon reading, and every couple of hours the boys brought good food for Quasimodo to sample while he whittled that block of wood. It was generally a quiet rainy after-noon in the attic. My kind of day.

Ophelia kept looking up from the pages of her novel to gaze at Quasimodo, feeling more sorrow for a person than she'd ever felt in her fourteen long years. This is called empathy, or the ability to put yourself in another person's shoes. If you can do this, then you are a much better human being than those who cannot. And that is all I have to say about that!

You see, despite the fact that Quasimodo found himself in the stocks because Deacon Frollo (his stepfather) forced Quasi to help him kidnap Esmeralda the Gypsy girl (obviously an unsuccessful venture), Esmeralda had just given Quasi a drink of water.

And now he was in love.

Poor thing, thought Ophelia, knowing that beautiful Gypsy girls never fall in love with monstrous versions of humanity like Quasimodo. Instead, girls like Esmeralda fall for dashing captains like Phoebus who don't give them the time of day or even the weather forecast, for that matter. Such young ladies often turned themselves into a sort of version of Quasimodo, only higher up on the "food chain" (those portions of society that deem themselves better than most people, typically a bit prettier, and generally possessing more money). Why a poor Gypsy girl thought a noble soldier like Phoebus would fall in love with her says something about her ego in an age in which all people were relegated (assigned, by birth in this instance) to a certain class of people. The admiration of the crowds must have sunk into her brain a bit too far.

Nevertheless, sometimes love stories between two people from different strata (levels) of society work out. But not usually. Ask any sociologist. *(And please, don't get me started about the sociology department at the university. Those people need to straighten up their act!)*

Ophelia sidled (walked casually) up to Linus in the kitchen as he was making another round of PB&Js. "Do you think we can change things for Quasi back in the Book World?"

"Huh?" He pulled out six pieces of bread from the bag.

"The imaginary realm." She handed him the peanut butter jar and a knife. "Make me one too, please."

He slid out two more slices and said nothing.

"Well, it's like this, Linus. Maybe we can tell Quasi the truth about Esmeralda. She's pretty and all, sure. But she'll never want anything to do with him. He should know that."

Linus shrugged. "Maybe."

"It's worth a try, right?"

"Sure."

She kissed him on the cheek. "Oh thank you, Linus," she said. "You're always so good to talk to."

"That's enough of that," Linus said, wiping his scarlet cheek again.

Ophelia walked to the window overlooking the street. "It's really coming down now. Do you know the forecast?"

"Rain. For the next three days."

"Yuck."

Uncle Augustus stepped into the kitchen. "How about one for me, Linus?"

Linus sighed and took two more slices of bread from the bag.

"Ah, looking at the rain I see. I spent many hours doing that when I was your age, Ophelia. Of course, we lived in Seattle at the time."

"I guess it was hard not to."

"Did you know that Kingscross is on a flood plain?" he asked.

She shook her head.

"Oh yes! We're due for a hundred-year flood, too. They say it can be terrible, and with that dam upriver ..."

"Maybe we should move stuff out of the basement." Linus could hardly believe he'd said the words. They'd just popped out of his practical brain when he wasn't thinking.

"Good idea! You kids do that. I'm sure you have nothing better to do today."

It was a job sneaking Quasimodo down to the basement, but nobody complained about the inconvenience. With his strong arm muscles and willingness to work hard, he was a great help. And he seemed glad for something to do. Walter was a big help as well, working up a sweat while Ophelia sat on an old chair the color of sidewalk gum and continued reading *The Hunchback of Notre-Dame*.

"You could help out a bit," Linus said to Ophelia after a poof of dust exploded in his face after he set down a half-open box of old-fashioned looking clothes.

"It's quite all right," Quasi said. "I'm more than happy to help.

And a fine lady such as Ophelia should not be subjected to heavy labor." Then he stammered, "What I mean to say, such a young lady should not be so burdened, that is," he said, growing redder by the minute, "no young miss should have to lift when there are strong young men around."

"Thank you Quasi," Ophelia said, turning rather pink herself. "I would help, but if you remember one of us needs to finish your book, and I don't believe anyone else has a start on it yet."

"How convenient," Linus smirked.

"See here!" Walter cried out, seemingly oblivious to the exchange, as he held up a box. "It's a box of books!"

They all groaned.

But nobody groaned an hour later when Walter discovered a box full of memorabilia. He picked up object after object.

"Look, Ophelia."

She arose from her chair and leaned over the box. "Oh my!" One by one she picked up what seemed to be Juliet's cap, Macbeth's broadsword, and the dagger Brutus might have used to slay Julius Caesar. "It's like treasures from the mind of William Shakespeare!" The three of them continued to rifle through the contents.

Then the boys pulled out more intriguing boxes labeled *The Canterbury Tales*, *The Three Musketeers*, *The Iliad*, *The Odyssey*, and more. Ten other boxes.

Ophelia met Linus's eyes.

Cato Grubbs, the mad scientist of the enchanted circle, was alive and well. And obviously he was a very busy man. Or was he? Could it be Cato, or perhaps someone else? Who could know?

A further conversation with Aunt Portia and Uncle Augustus was most definitely in order! Maybe they possessed more information about the former owner of the house than they were letting on.

"Did you see that?" asked Walter.

"See what?" Ophelia said.

"I thought I saw a shadow over there, in the corner by the furnace."

Linus shook his head. "Sorry."

Quasi set down a box on the bottom step. "I did, Walter. It looked like a man."

"A rather fat man?" asked Walter.

"Yes."

"I wonder who it could be?" Walter reached for another box to carry upstairs.

"Let's hope it's nobody," said Ophelia. "Let's hope there's a reasonable explanation for whatever you saw."

Later that afternoon, they were back upstairs listening to the rain. Walter couldn't stand being cooped up any longer. "Let's take a quick walk to the river," he said. "Surely we can get Quasi there and back without any trouble."

"I've got to read," said Ophelia, lying comfortably on Linus's bed.

"It's still raining," said Linus, doing some sort of calculation on the wall by the door.

"Then it's on me. Right," said Walter. "You mind a little rain?" he asked Quasi.

"No, I don't."

"I'll run interference for you," Ophelia offered. She hurried down the steps to the bookshop's office and engaged Aunt Portia in a conversation about literary fantasy. Uncle Auggie was out for the afternoon, headed to an estate sale in search of more books.

Walter hurried out the front door of the shop, side by side with Quasimodo.

"Are you sure this is all right?" asked Quasi, his gait rambling and crablike due to his severely bowed legs.

"Absolutely."

They ambled through the stone pillared gateway at the entrance to the park and made for the river.

Of course, a boy like Quasi, especially when he's clad in a pirate costume, can be only so inconspicuous. As Quasi and Walter strolled past a group of teenagers playing touch football, the young men stopped what they were doing and stared.

Then one cupped a hand beside his mouth and hollered, "Trick or treat!"

"Great costume!" yelled another.

The group now approached Walter and Quasimodo, and their apparent leader stepped forward. Walter knew how to size up a group, and he knew you always went for the toughest guy, if it came down to it. He quickly did the math. This guy was bigger than he was, but also fatter. Walter could take him if he had to. He'd just have to work a little harder.

Walter extended a hand. "I'm Walter."

"And, oh dear, dahling, I'm Briiii—an," he said in an awful imitation of a British accent. "Who's the freak and where did he get that mask? It's the ugliest thing I've ever seen."

Quasi looked down and shuffled his feet.

The last thing Walter wanted was a fight. He motioned Brian to come a little closer. "It's not a mask. And do you see the size of his hands?" he whispered. "He's as mean as he looks, too."

Brian quickly stepped back, pointed at Quasi, and said, "What a loser."

"Yeah," the others muttered.

"Let's get back to the game."

Walter breathed a sigh of relief. He could fight, but he usually let his mouth do everything it could to prevent it. Another success!

They continued on down the path a ways, and then Quasi asked, "What's a 'freak'? What's a 'loser'? Although, I think I can figure that one out. But what did I lose? Does he know something I don't?"

"No, Quasi. He doesn't know a thing. That lad is a brainless Neanderthal."

"What's a 'Neanderthal'?"

They sat down on a park bench overlooking the river as the rain continued falling in a light mist.

Good, thought Walter, a change of topic. He jumped on it.

eleven

Will the Real Cato Grubbs
Please Stand Up?

Aunt Portia had decided to go with a pea green theme for tea-time, which brought a grimace to Ophelia's lips. The theme should have been orange, since Portia generally tripped her culinary way along the light spectrum. But she was preoccupied by the rain falling nonstop for the past six hours. Forty-two hours and counting until they ushered Quasimodo back into the circle and back home to the Cathedral of Notre-Dame.

Ophelia worried about finishing the novel by then. She read quickly, to be sure. Nevertheless, she thought she might give reading at the dinner table a go. Better to be safe than sorry when someone's life is in your hands. Oh, the pressure!

Uncle Augustus cleared his throat and settled his cutlery in the proper position. "Ophelia, darling. This isn't a library, you know."

"But it's just so good, Uncle Auggie!"

"Be that as it may, dinnertime is a social time, not a necessary evil."

"Teatime," corrected Aunt Portia.

Linus, loving food the way he did, had to agree. He nodded once in his uncle's general direction, and they exchanged that man-to-man expression that Ophelia and Portia despised.

The females shook their heads. Ophelia laid the book aside and began eating her pea soup. Coming up next was pea salad, of course, followed by some kind of pea spread on crackers. Thankfully, no pea-flavored crackers could be found on the shelves of any grocery store.

Aunt Portia had outdone herself.

"It certainly doesn't look good down by the river," said Uncle Augustus as he spooned up his soup against the far side of the bowl.

Aunt Portia picked up a cracker and bit off the end of it. "The rain isn't supposed to let up for days. It's ten years too soon, you know."

"Too soon for what?" Linus asked.

"The hundred-year flood. The dam up by Joan Dawson's farm has needed repairing for years. They were supposed to start working on it in July, when the water gets low," said Aunt Portia. (Joan, a soybean farmer, was surprisingly well read and came into the bookshop at least once a week.)

"Uh-oh," said Linus, "you don't think ..."

"Unfortunately, I do. If this rain doesn't slow down ..."

"Let's just hope and pray the dam holds," said Uncle Augustus. "We've had this much rain before, and it's always been fine."

Ever the pessimist (a person who sees situations in their most negative light), Portia narrowed her eyes. "Let's hope so. And thank you, children, for getting all of that flotsam and jetsam (various bits of junk and useless items) out of the basement. I've been meaning to go through it for years."

"Speaking of junk in the basement," Ophelia jumped on the topic, "can you tell us more about Cato Grubbs? We found some of his lab equipment down there. Is he dead?"

Portia leaned forward. (She's always loved a little harmless gossip. Oh the things she's told me that I'll never tell you!) "Nobody knows if he died or not, dear. He simply disappeared one day. And when he didn't come back for six months, his attorney put the house on the market. He said if we took the contents of the house as well, we could have it for a discount."

"Guess Mr. Grubbs's possessions didn't have much value."

"No. And rightfully so." Uncle Augustus leaned forward and said in a low voice, "I didn't get a good feeling around most of it."

Ophelia would have tapped her temple with her forefinger if she hadn't cared about giving away the secret of the enchanted circle. "Did all of it go down to the basement then?"

"Oh no," Portia said. "Most of it went out the door. All except the books, that is. It was just a lot of junk, as far as I was concerned. Burners and jars and cans and the like. I must have just missed one of the boxes of lab equipment. We kept all of the clothes though."

Linus raised an eyebrow.

"Oh quite right!" Uncle Augustus exclaimed. "Those items formed the beginning of my costume collection."

"And nobody's ever heard from him?" Ophelia asked as the rain began tapping against the kitchen windows more insistently.

"Not a soul. He had no relatives to speak of. But there was talk that he'd moved to South America and is now doing science as a sidewalk magic act for tourists — things smoking and exploding and disappearing and such."

"Sounds terrible," said Ophelia.

Sounds terrific, thought Linus.

"Did he leave any pictures behind?" Ophelia asked.

"One," said Uncle Augustus. "I'll fetch it for you after dinner."

"Tea," corrected Aunt Portia.

"Yes, dear sister."

Cato has to be alive, Ophelia surmised, *and he's using the base ment as his storage space*.

Quasimodo learned quickly. He took one look at the leftovers from the pea fest and asked for a PB&J sandwich. He ate these sandwiches as though the end of the world drew nigh (near); but considering the instability of the dam upriver, the end of Kingscross sure seemed to be a distinct possibility. At any rate, Quasi knew he was headed back to Paris, a city without a single peanut. He wondered if he could return to that bleak life without going insane.

They all sat around Linus's room after tea. Walter was there too, and he did nothing but complain about his meal next door: Mystery meat, instant mashed potatoes, and reheated frozen corn that was watery and flaccid (limp), just sitting there in a plastic food storage tub.

Quasimodo felt sorry for Walter and asked if he'd like to have a PB&J, too.

"No thanks, Quasi. You're a real sport." He plopped down on Linus's bed. "Have you all been to the river? It's rising."

"So I hear," Ophelia yawned from her perch on Linus's beanbag chair and then turned another page in her book.

Try not to be too hard on her. They moved to Kingscross from Arizona, so she couldn't possibly understand the implications of a flood.

Suddenly, Opehlia sat up straight. "So Quasi, tell me about Esmeralda."

Quasimodo closed his good eye. "Oh my, Ophelia. She's pretty, like you. And she dances so beautifully. She gave me water, you know, that day at the stocks—right before I ended up in the enchanted circle."

"I know all that. That's what the book says. But I want to know what you like about her—other than the fact that she was nice to you."

He squinted. It seemed an odd question. A pretty girl helps you out—what more does a person need to know? "I don't understand."

"I mean, you really like her, don't you? You've pretty much fallen head over heels for the young lady, right?"

He nodded. "I suppose so, if head over heels means 'thoroughly.'"

"And Deacon Frollo has fallen for her too."

"Yes," he sighed. "And that complicates matters. Not to mention the fact that he's a priest. But he did save my life, Ophelia. I can never forget that."

"So what's the big deal? She has a kind heart and light feet and a little goat. Cool. But is she smart? Is she steady and brave? Do you think she'd come to love a boy like you? I mean really?"

He didn't care for the direction of this conversation. "I haven't really thought about it all that deeply. Of course I don't think she'll ever come to love me. I mean, who would when I look like this?"

"I didn't mean that, Quasi." Ophelia so wished he could stay in Real World (as she'd come to think of it) a while longer. She would usher him to a plastic surgeon, have that wart removed, and then see what could be done about his back. A good haircut might work wonders too. "But if you feel that way, why bother to get all dreamy-eyed about her? You're only asking for trouble down the road."

"Sometimes it's good to feel something just for the sake of feeling, Ophelia." Quasimodo picked up the block of wood he'd been whittling into a little pony with a tiny princess on its back. "Not everything has to have a successful outcome to be considered a worthy pursuit."

Ouch. Ophelia had failed to credit Quasimodo for having much depth. "Where do you come up with thoughts like that?"

"You'd be surprised how many ideas will come to you when you're alone and all is silent."

Linus nodded vigorously. Ophelia and Walter looked at each other, pure wonderment at such a thought stitching their minds together for a few seconds.

Quasimodo continued, "People have always assumed that my outward deformities cut through to the center of my brain. I'm a human being, Ophelia. Just like everybody else. If I desire to experience human emotion in all its fullness—sorrow as well as joy—then isn't that my choice?"

"It's true," said Linus.

Well, that didn't work out so well, Ophelia thought before returning to the story. She'd been hoping to undermine Quasimodo's feelings for Esmeralda. It would sure save him a wagonload of trouble later on in the book if what happened now in Real World could change future events in Book World. It might even save his life.

"Besides," said Quasi, "Deacon Frollo would never allow anything to happen between us even if she did come to care about me ... which she won't."

"What's he like?" asked Linus.

"He used to be a bit less ... how do I put it? Driven. Now it's as if a certain madness has come upon him." Quasi looked over his shoulder. "I shouldn't speak about him like this."

"Do you think it's the alchemy?" Walter asked.

"Maybe," said Quasi. "He locks himself in his room for days and days. He's obsessed with his experiments. But I have no place else to go. The Cathedral is the only place for someone like me."

Ophelia wasn't so sure about that.

twelve

Funny, I Never Pictured a Mad Scientist Looking Like That

𝔍t had to happen sooner or later. Close calls are like that. "Some-one's coming up the steps!" Walter hissed as he shot up from his seat. "Quasi, quick! Sit in the beanbag chair."

Quasi complied, and the footsteps got louder as Uncle Augustus made his way down the hall. They were a clunk-clunk kind of footstep, not Aunt Portia's click-click variety. And they were slower too, as if the person were ambling down the boardwalk in Atlantic City, or walking along the shop fronts with his hands in his pockets.

"Hurry!" Walter grabbed a heap of Linus's dirty clothing that had been tossed in a corner.

"Sorry, Quasi," whispered Ophelia as the first armful fell in his lap.

"It's all right," he whispered back as they piled more clothing on top of him.

This was one time when Linus's propensity to procrastinate (tendency to put off until another day or time) doing his laundry actually served a good purpose. Normally, I wouldn't recommend such tactics with one's personal linens. They sit in the corner and broadcast all sorts of unhealthy microbes, spores, and germs—you can be sure of that. If you should ever fall ill because of it, you have only yourself to blame. You have been forewarned, leaving me for-ever off the hook (not responsible) for your overall state of health.

As the doorknob turned, Ophelia dove back onto the bed and

picked up her book, Linus pretended he was looking through his desk drawer, and Walter dropped to the floor and started doing push-ups.

"Ah, well then!" Uncle Augustus stepped into the room. "Look at you young people! You are industrious and model citizens even on your own time. Very good!"

"Thanks, Uncle Auggie." Ophelia yawned and stretched. "Oh man. You can really get stiff if you lay in the same position for too long."

Walter stood to his feet. "That's right, Ophelia. You should do push-ups with me next time."

"I agree," said Linus.

Ophelia flipped the pages of the paperback like a deck of cards as a nervous laugh escaped. "That's us—ever the responsible ones!"

"I say," said Walter. "What brings you here to see us, sir?"

Could we be acting any less normal? thought Linus. Thankfully, Uncle Augustus was already preoccupied with his next party. "What do you think about the theme for my next gala: "A Whale of a Tale Water Party." Guests wear their bathing suits or come dressed as a character from *Moby-Dick*. I'm unsure about the name, though. And do you think I can borrow enough sprinklers to add some water to the mix?"

"But Uncle Augustus," Ophelia said, glancing nervously at the pile of dirty clothes. "People can't sit around in bathing suits eating seafood. I mean, what sane person would want to see such a thing?"

"Well, it isn't until next month," Uncle Augustus replied. "But I wanted you to be thinking up some good ideas. Children have such wonderful imaginations. Anyway, here's the picture of Cato Grubbs that you requested." He held out a yellowed photo, a formal portrait that looked to have been taken in the 1920s. "Enjoy. If you can."

Linus took it from him.

Uncle Augustus turned to Walter. "Walter, are you spending the night with us?"

"Oh no, sir. I'll just stick around for a little while longer. Until all the snacks are gone."

Uncle Augustus chuckled and left the room, closing the door behind him. Ophelia let out a blustery sigh just as he popped his head back into the room. They all jumped a bit. "Oh, and Linus, I think it's time for you to do some laundry. Tomorrow. Chop-chop." He pointed to a pair of leather shoes peeking out from the bottom of the pile. "And return those shoes to the wardrobe room. The party is over, after all."

Ophelia sighed again after Uncle Auggie had closed the door a second time. "Oh my goodness! That was nerve-racking."

"Sorry about my feet." Quasimodo pushed the clothing aside. "I don't see what the problem is with these clothes. Why do they need to be washed?"

Ophelia held her nose. "Because things smell worse more quickly these days."

"These aren't smelly. Or, actually, they're not very smelly," he said.

"Okay, Linus, let's see this Cato Grubbs," Ophelia said.

Linus turned on the desk lamp and set the picture underneath the beam of light.

Walter whistled. "Certainly not what I expected."

"Me either," Ophelia shook her head.

You got that right, Linus thought.

"He looks like a very nice man," said Quasimodo.

Quasi must not have good eyesight, Linus figured, because the portrait of Cato did not depict a nice man at all.

Now, if you're picturing the tall, dark-haired villainous sort of … well, villain, with a fiery glint in his eyes and a cruel twist to his mouth, then you're thinking of someone quite the opposite of Cato Grubbs. Fat, blond, and smooth-skinned, he was dressed in a rather flamboyant (bold and showy) manner. He wore a cravat (silk scarf) tied around his neck, and on his hands were several rings — a pinky ring in particular supported a very large diamond. Linus wondered from which novel Cato had taken it.

Cato didn't exactly look like the picture of kind respectability either — just a nice, eccentric owner of the laboratory supply shop around the corner. He just didn't sport the sinister appearance that one might expect. Except for one thing.

"His eyes," said Ophelia. "I don't trust them."

Cold and calculating, thought Linus.

Walter agreed, "Looks like he'd turn on you for a meat pie."

Quasi screwed up his face. "I can't see that at all."

"Have you ever seen him before?" asked Ophelia.

Quasi scratched his cheek and stared at the photo. "No. I'd remember him if I had."

I must be reading Cato's copy of the book, thought Ophelia.

"I don't like his mouth," said Walter. "It looks a bit too willing to be nice, if you know what I mean."

"Disingenuous (false or hypocritical). He's definitely projecting a certain image." Ophelia leaned over and took a closer look. "I wonder when this photo was taken?"

Long ago, thought Linus. It made him wonder what Mr. Grubbs looked like today. Was he elderly and decrepit? Or did living in books suspend not only time, but also the aging process? Was staying young the original motivation (reason) for Cato's experiments? Or did he just stumble upon it by accident one night during a thunderstorm worthy of Dr. Frankenstein?

"We'd better be careful," Walter said. "If he's still using the attic, then we're probably getting in his way."

Ophelia put down the photo. "You're right! I hadn't thought of that. Perhaps he's just letting this thing with Quasi play out and assumes we'll be done with the attic after that."

He sure doesn't know you then, thought Linus.

"Let's hope so," Walter said from his seat on the floor. "Maybe next time you'll be more careful at 11:11, Ophelia."

Ophelia cocked an eyebrow. "Really? I have the opportunity to meet book characters in the flesh, and I'm not going to jump on that? I don't think so, Walter."

He began doing sit-ups. "Good girl."

Ophelia smiled.

"Right, then. The street's deserted," Walter said. "Let's go!"

Ophelia settled a thick shawl over Quasimodo's head and shoulders, and the group rushed across the street to the church. With Ophelia and Walter taking the lead, the two of them leaped over the small pools that had collected in the potholes, Quasimodo sloshed right through them, and Linus easily stepped over them with his long legs.

Walter looked out upon the rainy street and wondered why he had the good fortune to end up in an adventure like this one. He hadn't wanted to come to America to attend high school, and certainly not spend the entire summer there ahead of time; but it was turning out for the best. Jessica, his mum, always said that life does that—turns out for the best—but he'd failed to believe her before now. When Auntie Max had told Walter about the school in Kingscross and her willingness to pay for him to attend there, Jessica Liddel had jumped at the offer.

"Just think of it, Walt," she'd said. "A good education at a good school. Never, never, never could we have afforded such a thing on our own."

His mum's words had overflowed with such hope that Walter would have rather dog-paddled across the English Channel than disappoint her. After all, it had always been just Walter and his mum, and he tried his utmost to keep it that way.

The wind drove the rain at them from the right and at such an angle that an umbrella (had they possessed one, which they did not) would have been rendered useless.

None of them thought about practical things like umbrellas or the proper gear for inclement (nasty) weather. Nowadays children receive no instruction on that sort of thing. Oh no! Better to be wet and look like a soaked dog than to carry about an umbrella or, heaven help us, pull on a pair of those awful galoshes that you can easily remove at the door to keep from dragging mud and muck all throughout the building. (*If you think galoshes are part of a Hungarian meal, then tough luck. You shall have to look up the real meaning of the term on your own. I am doing this on principle, you see.*)

Walter led them on a brick pathway that hugged the left side of the church. Rhododendrons lined the other side. They walked to the back of the stone building, and Walter shone the flashlight on the cornerstone that said 1877. They stopped before a door that was painted the standard church-door crimson color. Walter grasped the handle and pressed down the latch with his thumb. Good. It gave way and he silently pushed the door inward.

Ophelia followed him. "I'm glad Father Wellborne remembered."

"I'm glad he didn't know we can't see Jupiter on a night like tonight," said Walter.

Linus wiped his feet on the mat. "Right."

Ophelia didn't comment on the ludicrous (laughable) nature of their excuse. No sense in doing that now.

Quasi shut the door behind him, removed the shawl from his head, and looked around. He inhaled deeply through his nose and sighed. "They all smell basically the same, don't they? These old churches?"

Ophelia touched his arm. "Are you glad we came?"

"Yes. This makes me feel a little better inside."

"Let's go." Walter pointed the flashlight beam toward a set of narrow, circular stone steps. "These go up to the bell tower."

Walter, then Ophelia, then Quasimodo, then Linus, ascended the steep staircase.

"The bell tower doesn't look this high from the street," complained Ophelia. The steps seemed to go on and on.

The door at the top of the staircase was unlocked as well, and they soon stood inside the square room at the top of the tower. The twins were out of breath, while Walter and Quasimodo were doing just fine.

Linus aimed the flashlight up toward the ceiling, illuminating the four bells.

Quasi, bending back at the waist, looked up. "They're quite small."

"Large enough to make the neighbors complain," said Ophelia.

Quasi laughed and nodded with his whole body. "Oh yes! One of my favorite pastimes!" He turned to Ophelia. "Of course I couldn't hear them very well then. Do you think I can take these hearing aids back with me?"

Ophelia looked at Walter.

Walter shrugged. "These were just her spares. Madge already bought a new set—state of the art. Go right ahead."

Quasimodo reached up and touched a bell. "Thinner, smaller, but a bell nonetheless. Why are there ropes here if they are, as you say, automated?"

"Sometimes the electricity, or the power that runs them, goes out. So I guess they'd have to ring them the old-fashioned way," said Ophelia.

"That's good to know." Quasimodo continued to run his hands along the bell. He came upon a rope and tugged ever so lightly. The bell barely moved. "Yes, you're exactly right. They'll still work."

"It's all you can do not to pull that thing, isn't it?" asked Walter.

"It's taking everything in me not to."

None of them could really understand Quasimodo and the life he'd led before coming through the enchanted circle, how he could love bells that much. But that didn't seem to matter. They only had to be his friends and help him out. It was a good feeling, really.

And we get to have this little adventure in the process, Walter thought, silently thanking Auntie Max for the opportunity that he'd been cursing only days before. Perhaps his mum knew what she was talking about after all. Imagine that!

(If you, dear parent, are reading this book along with your child and are now feeling a bit inflated by Walter's words, then go put a pin in your big head. You know you'll mess up again. And, most likely, it'll be quite soon.)

They sat right under the bells, the darkness and the sound of rain enclosing them in their own small universe.

Linus shone the flashlight on his wristwatch. "It's now 11:11," he said.

"Twenty-four hours gone," said Ophelia.

"Thirty-six hours left," Quasi said, his voice overflowing with sadness. "It's so much better here."

"Cheer up, mate. We'll make this the best thirty-six hours of your life." Walter slapped him on the back. "So tell us about bell ringing. We're simply dying to know."

"It seems ridiculous to say it out loud, but the bells are my friends." Quasimodo crossed his legs and leaned back on his hands. "They never question anything I do. And we're a team. When I pull the ropes, they respond—and with such enthusiasm! Then I become happier, and round and round it goes." He paused. "I learned more from the bells than any human ever taught me. Treat something with love and respect, and it will join you in making something beautiful."

Linus inhaled through his nose and felt a sadness overcome him.

"Why that's lovely, Quasi," said Ophelia.

Just then at the top of the stairwell, a head appeared. It was covered in hair so white that it rendered the flashlight beam unnecessary. Nobody had heard the man climbing the steps. They had come to the tower under false pretenses, most certainly; and now it seemed they'd been caught.

thirteen

Who Says Bounty Hunters Don't Make Good Priests?

"What's up, you guys?" the deep voice attached to the white hair said. "What a terrible night to see Jupiter, and yet look at you! You must have some high-tech equipment to be able to see through cloud cover as thick as this stuff."

"Hello, Father Wellborne," said Walter, his voice dropping.

"I'll bet you didn't know I'm somewhat of an amateur astronomer myself."

Linus sighed. Figures. Here we are trying to do someone a good turn, and we get caught lying. Just our luck.

"Okay, Walter. Introduce me to your friends." Father Wellborne paused and then pointed at Walter. "You weren't doing anything illegal, were you?"

"No!"

"All right."

Linus had a good feeling about this man. He wondered if it might be wise to share the secret of the enchanted circle with an adult, particularly one who wasn't in the family, didn't assign their chores, didn't expect them to get As in school, and didn't eat meals with them every day. After all, Father Wellborne could drive, buy a bottle of brandy in case someone ended up with a gaping wound, and give them advice whenever necessary. Add to that the fact that they could outrun him if need be, and he was about as safe a bet as anyone out there—more so, actually.

Linus was just learning to trust his intuition. You see, Father

Wellborne heeded the call to the ministry later in life. Before that, he'd worked as a bounty hunter (someone who's unafraid to track down and capture dangerous people who are wanted by the law, and who will most likely win the fight when said dangerous people refuse to accompany him to the police station). Besides astronomy, Father Wellborne also loved martial arts and fine tea. And he read voraciously (with great hunger). Talk about coming in handy! And if you figured in his regular prayers and his connection to the Almighty, then Father Wellborne would make a stellar addition to the team.

"We have a confession to make, sir," Linus said.

Walter sucked in his breath, while Ophelia's high-pitched laugh spelled out the words, I-A-M-N-E-R-V-O-U-S!

Father Wellborne's hearty laugh split the dark. "We're not that kind of church."

Linus inhaled deeply. "No. It's about what we're doing here right now. Ophelia, you tell him."

She cleared her throat. "Well, we were all reading about velocity when we thought, 'Hey, why not drop things from the bell tower and see how fast they fall?' So here we are ...?"

Linus said, "Not that story! The truth."

"The truth?" Ophelia's mouth gaped.

Walter stood up tall. "What? We didn't discuss this as a collective. Maybe Quasimo—"

"Quasimodo?" Father Wellborne interrupted. He turned on his flashlight. "Is that the silent member of your group? Step forward, son. By the way, you guys, it isn't nice to call somebody 'Quasimo'—." The rector stopped in mid-sentence as the flashlight illuminated Quasimodo's face. "Hey. You weren't kidding, were you?" He flashed the beam of light at each of them in turn. "This is either some Halloween costume or else you've got some serious explaining to do."

"Halloween costume?" asked Quasi.

"Never mind!" the trio said in unison.

"Wow!" said Father Wellborne. "Sorry I said anything."

"Oh, we'll be glad to explain." Walter took the priest's arm. "How about we share our story over a cup of tea?"

"I'm game if you are. By the way, call me Father Lou. I'm not a very formal kind of guy."

Linus figured as much. He'd thought all priests wore black and called people "my child." Boy, was he glad to be wrong about that!

Back at Father Lou's manse (the house and land occupied by a minister), Ophelia received a warm mug of tea from the rector with both hands.

"Just start at the beginning," he said.

They all sat around his kitchen table as the skies continued to hurl down the rain in sheets (and blankets and pillows, for that matter). Yes, it was that bad. Noah would have been ready to close up the door of the ark by this point.

Ophelia, with punctuations by Walter and an occasional illustration by Quasimodo, told the tale. Linus nodded appropriately.

At the end of the story, Father Lou sat back and blew through his mouth. "So you're telling me this is the real hunchback of Notre-Dame, so to speak." He turned to Quasimodo. "And what you say is true?"

"Yes, Father."

Father Lou poured himself another cup of tea. "You know, I thought I'd seen everything. And believe me, I've seen everything. But apparently I haven't seen everything."

Ophelia sat up straight. "You believe us?"

He took a sip. "Look at this fellow. There's no way that's a costume."

"And you won't tell anybody?" asked Walter.

"Of course not. Who'd believe me anyway?"

"I'm certain. I'd know those feet anywhere!" Quasimodo sat fidgeting on the blue sofa, clearly agitated and out of breath from the fright. "I don't know why I thought he'd never find me."

As they were running home from Father Lou's manse (a charming little stone cottage that was really the last place anybody who was ever a bounty hunter should be living), they'd noticed two figures rounding the corner of the boarding house, er, school, and walking from Rickshaw Street onto Havisham Way. The streetlamp revealed the tall and thin one was wearing a dark cloak, while the short and squat one was dressed in a rather dandified (a bit too frilly for a man) manner. Even wet, Cato Grubbs was clearly the fancy one. So it stood to reason that the cloak and the very thin, long feet belonged to Deacon Frollo.

One has never seen feet quite so skewed in the length to width ratio. And Quasi, whose posture affords him a good view of the knees-down mostly, could certainly be trusted to recognize any pair of feet he'd seen on such a regular basis. You can be sure that if he said it was Frollo, then it was Frollo.

Now back up in the attic, their hair drying after enduring an even harder rain shower than when they'd left for the bell tower, Ophelia handed Quasi a PB&J. "Why would he be looking for you? You'd think he'd be just as glad to have all of that attention off of you, the Cathedral, and himself."

Walter made himself a sandwich. "I don't know the story very well, but it seems to me this Frollo chap doesn't care much for the Cathedral or for Quasi. Now himself? That's another story altogether."

If someone could take a mournful bite of a sandwich, Quasimodo did so just then. Ophelia wanted to cry. Imagine being so alone. And it made no difference which reality you inhabited, you simply had to survive without a family or people who knew you so well that they knew what you were thinking before you thought it. Though her parents had always been self-absorbed, at least she'd always had Linus. She realized that her parents siring (giving birth to) twins was nothing short of divine intervention, because having to fend for oneself in a household like that would have been a recipe for an oddness so intense, one might never recover from it for the rest of one's life.

I tend to agree with her. Although there were times when I wished my mother and father would just go away, that happened only occasionally. And mostly during the junior high years. I would not go back to those days unless someone threatened to roll me around in a vat of germs. Some things are worse than that space between childhood and adulthood. Yet it's almost impossible to see that at the time. So if you frequently feel sorry for yourself, just picture somebody throwing you into a barrel of slime and maybe that will make you feel better. Good heavens, I feel like I should go wash my hands now.

Quasimodo had no one. As quickly as they'd all become friends, neither Ophelia nor Walter nor Linus were like a sibling to Quasi, or that school friend who saved you a seat at lunch from the time you were in kindergarten until you graduated from high school.

Quasimodo swallowed a bite of sandwich. "Frollo took me in. I can never forget that."

Ophelia replied, "He also made you grab Esmeralda, Quasi, so he could take her for himself! And then you ended up in the stocks! He didn't step forward and take the blame for that—even though it was clearly his fault. He's a lily-livered coward. You shouldn't forget that, either."

Note Ophelia's use of the word lily-livered, a very antiquated phrase. She was being a bit redundant (unnecessarily repetitive) here because she literally called Frollo a "cowardly coward." But this is dialogue; people say stupid things like that all the time, so a writer can get away with it. It helps develop a character better when their speech is their own—even if it is repetitive.

"So Frollo is a priest?" asked Linus.

Quasimodo nodded.

"Was he ever sincere?" asked Ophelia, sitting beside the enchanted circle and grabbing a sandwich for herself.

"When he was younger, yes. I don't know if the person he's become would have adopted a monstrous little—"

"Don't say that!" interrupted Ophelia.

"Well, an orphan like me. He was very pious (holy). But then things started to change."

"The alchemy?" Ophelia asked.

Quasimodo nodded.

During the Middle Ages, the time from which Quasimodo had been snatched, as well as in centuries before that, some men displayed an intense interest in something called alchemy. People searched for ways to turn everyday matter into gold using the creation of the philosopher's stone. And they also sought for ways to live excruciatingly long lives because, let's be honest, not enough troubles and germs exist in one normal lifetime. In short, some folks tried to create supernatural happenings using everyday materials.

Nowadays most people look at that as sinister and, simply put, impossible (although there are a few who beg to differ). Suffice it to say, their knowledge of science was not as advanced. The periodic table of elements that tells us iron could never become gold did not exist then. Gold is; iron is. Both are what they are at their most basic level, and that is that. In other words, they are not like salt, which contains two elements—sodium and chlorine—or water, which has both hydrogen and oxygen. Certainly you see what I mean. If not, then count yourself as one of the dullards and please do not come study in my English department. Thank you.

Quasimodo clenched his hands together. "Frollo became different when he began locking himself away in his study for weeks at a time. He could see the Gypsy girl from the window too."

"That didn't help matters," Walter said.

Ophelia said, "Why would he want to come here? To find you, obviously. But why does he need to find you?"

Linus, of course, had an idea. But he kept it to himself for now.

"I'd better get back to reading." Ophelia sighed.

The guys decided they might as well get a good night's sleep. Ophelia figured she'd stay on the blue sofa again and keep guard over Quasimodo. Most likely nobody would be coming through the enchanted circle tonight. Not if they were already here.

Ophelia crept downstairs, checked the locks on all the windows, made sure the doors were bolted (Portia and Augustus, two all-too-trusting souls, sometimes forgot to do this), and hoped and prayed that Frollo and Cato would wait until daylight to make their next move. Whatever that was going to be.

Around 3:00 a.m., Quasimodo tugged on Ophelia's arm, awakening her with a start.

"What?" she cried out.

"Shhh! Look!"

Quasi pointed to the table where the wooden carving of the dancing woman was trying to unseat the princess on the horse. "My carvings!" he whispered with urgency. "They're alive!"

Ophelia couldn't believe what she was seeing. "Should we intervene?"

Quasimodo shook his head and gave an exaggerated shrug.

"Let's just see what happens," said Ophelia.

The dancer had a good hold on the princess's arm, but the regal horsewoman was having none of it. She cocked a booted foot, placed it on the dancer's chest, and gave a mighty shove. The girl went tumbling head over feet, and the princess galloped off behind the beakers.

The dancer then rolled into a ball and hardened back to her wooden state.

Quasimodo picked her up. "Oh, the poor girl."

"Is it Esmeralda?" Ophelia asked.

"Yes."

"I suppose that fight was about Captain Phoebus?" she asked.

"She's in love with him, isn't she? She really is."

"He'll be her downfall, Quasimodo. Don't let Esmeralda be yours."

Ophelia looked for the princess on the worktable, but she and her horse were gone.

fourteen

Thereby Proving That All Scientists Are Mad Scientists

And If You Don't Like That, Take It Up with the Administration

Dear Linus and Ophelia,

It was good to get your letter telling us that we chose wisely in sending you to visit Aunt Portia and Uncle Augustus. What fun those two old birds can be if you're in the right frame of mind for their type. And when you're not, just think of your father and me, and that will help most certainly.

Ophelia snorted at that last part. *They have no idea*, she thought. She continued reading:

Our work here on Willis is slowgoing, though we expected nothing less. When you've been doing what we've been doing for this many years, the expectations become more realistic. We do hope you're heeding our advice to eat well, get plenty of sleep, and keep reading up on butterflies. It will give us something to talk about when we get home in five years.

Ophelia rolled her eyes. Talk about unrealistic expectations. Nothing but scientific jargon spilled onto the stationery from there on. It was Ophelia's second time reading the letter from her mother. But she wasn't reading it for sentimental reasons; she just needed a break from *The Hunchback of Notre-Dame*, and Quasi had finally fallen back asleep.

The story was too tragic. Tragic beyond belief. It would be one thing for such sadness to befall a person who'd been given much at birth. But poor Quasi was forced to deal with such misery after life had handed him what amounted to a plate piled high with turnips and rutabagas and cranberry sauce. It was too much to bear.

She knew it was only a novel. And she knew its author, Victor Hugo, employed drama quite masterfully in his writing. He enjoyed turning up the heat, so to speak, by taking an already terrible set of circumstances and throwing in someone who didn't deserve to deal with them. And while that plot device always makes for a good story, in real life it feels as if something in the universe has been tipped so far out of balance that only a miracle will right things again.

And that Esmeralda! Ophelia could barely read about such an empty-headed girl without wanting to throw the book out the trefoil window and into the rain. Times sure had changed, she realized. Not many readers would take to such a muttonhead (no offense to sheep) traipsing along the pages of a book. She could barely stand it.

"Thank goodness she didn't come through the circle," Ophelia muttered.

Quasimodo stirred. Ophelia rubbed his shoulder lightly, and he fell back into a deep slumber. She smiled as she remembered him telling her, just before he fell asleep, that he thought his favorite thing about Real World might be this wonderful mattress. And her, of course.

Having Quasimodo around helped Ophelia to see the many things she'd taken for granted all of her life, including her average face and body. After this experience, she never wanted to be more than what she was, I can assure you. For instance, she never dyed her hair, or plastered on makeup, or spent hours at the gym. Quasimodo taught her that she'd been given so much. He also taught her the beauty of gratitude, good health, and slipping through crowds unnoticed.

Around 4:30 a.m. an exhausted Ophelia opened her eyes for the first time in about ninety-three minutes. The smell of sulfur from a burning match had awakened her. She saw two figures now dominated the attic space—you can probably guess who they were—and they were whispering about how to get Quasimodo out of the building without disturbing the rest of the household.

Ophelia quickly closed her eyes and kept them closed. She hardly dared to breathe in order to hear their faint whispers more clearly.

"I fail to comprehend why we cannot return with Quasimodo right here," Frollo said.

Ophelia had never heard such a warm voice used in such a cool manner and with very little emotion evident.

That must be what his homilies sound like, she thought. (If you don't attend a church founded before the 1600s or thereabout, homily is simply a fancy word for "sermon.")

Frollo was much taller and thinner than Cato Grubbs, a rather corpulent (overweight) man who was even more corpulent up-close. The scientist had clearly gained weight over the years while traveling through the Book World.

Maybe the food tastes better over there, Ophelia thought, then shook herself mentally. Best to listen with a keen ear.

"This particular circle only works at 11:11 p.m. on the eleventh day of the month—coming, that is. Then, sixty hours later at 11:11 a.m., it opens up for the return passage."

"So limited," Frollo said with disgust.

"I got you here, didn't I?" Cato reprimanded as he swept an arm over the painted circle. "Be my guest then."

Frollo fumed and his breathing grew louder.

Cato looked through the powders. "In any case, we have to get Quasimodo back to the same portal that you and I came through. It's a better portal, actually. I use this attic just for storage now."

"And you are certain we can get him back to the exact place and time he disappeared?" Frollo asked.

"Fear not, Deacon Frollo. That won't be a problem."

"I'll be tried for witchcraft otherwise."

"So you've said many times. I'm sure it must have been frightening when that mob turned on you after your charge disappeared like a puff of smoke. It isn't a good place to be in, is it?"

Frollo seemed to understand Cato's moral lesson. "My being tried and hung for witchcraft and Quasimodo being jeered at by the crowd are two very different matters," he hissed.

"Of course they are," Cato muttered before changing the subject. "Just so we're clear about the matter—you'll be able to get Esmeralda's necklace for me before I return to this world?"

Ophelia felt the distrust in Cato's voice even from her spot on the sofa. She couldn't say she blamed him either.

"Yes. I have a very clear plan in place for her to willingly give it over to me."

I'll bet, thought Ophelia.

"Ah, here it is!" said Cato.

"So you have the powder?" Frollo asked.

"Here. Take it. You should find it most beneficial in your experiments."

Frollo said nothing, not even offering the common courtesy of a simple "Thank you."

"All right. Let's go to my lab. We'll come back here early in the morning and watch for them to leave. Then we'll get Quasimodo and take him back to my house for safekeeping."

"Why do we not just take him now?" asked Frollo.

Cato chuckled. "Why, look at us, dear deacon. I'm too fat; you're too skinny. Even between the two of us, we couldn't get that strong young man down two flights of steps with three teenagers and two adults fighting us as well. And then the priest across the street will surely hear the ensuing ruckus—"

"Quasimodo will obey me."

Ophelia risked a small peek. Frollo's eyes blazed.

"After what you did to him? Don't count on it. At the very least, I'm not counting on it, so what I say goes in this world. Is that understood, Deacon?"

Frollo said nothing and turned to exit the room.

Cato placed another canister, one holding a stash of Dragon-well Lung Ching tea, into his brown leather satchel (small bag with a shoulder strap), muttering, "I need to lose some weight."

Outside, the rainfall increased. The staccato on the roof now sounded more like running horses than the pitter-patter of little feet. "And let's hope the weather doesn't make our return to your world impossible."

Cato loved keeping current on the weather and such. He'd seen rain like this before. And he was smart enough to know that if it failed to slow down soon, then things might get messy indeed. "Oh, how I wish he hadn't tagged along after me," Cato whispered as he passed the sofa and headed out the door. "But now that I'm stuck with him, I might as well use him."

After the men had left, Ophelia waited five minutes and then ran downstairs to wake up Linus.

She told him what had happened. "And just so you know who we're dealing with, Cato isn't a nice man at all, Linus. He's asked Frollo to give him Esmeralda's emerald necklace—which is the only thing she has from the mother she never knew—as payment for bringing Frollo across to the Real World. Isn't that terrible?"

"Why did Frollo have to come?"

"He wants to make sure that Quasi reappears in the exact same moment he left Book World so Frollo won't be tried for witchcraft."

Linus rubbed his face with the hem of his T-shirt. "Let's get Walt."

"Do you know how to sneak over to the school?"

"Yep."

"Do you know which room is Walter's?"

"Yep."

"How come I don't know?" She felt left out.

"You've been doing a lot of reading lately."

"Oh. Right. Let's go."

fifteen

Sometimes Fourteen Years of Life Experience Clearly Has Its Disadvantages

𝒞he floors at the Kingscross School for Young People deserved an award for high achievement in squeaking, groaning, and even some vociferous (loud or clamorous) popping noises now and then. One board in particular sounded like a canine's sad cry. But despite the building's protests at a pre-dawn invasion by the ruffians next door, Linus and Ophelia made it to Walter's room without discovery. Perhaps the fact that Madrigal Pierce slept without her hearing aids contributed to their success as well.

In any case, Walter agreed that Quasimodo needed to be moved and quickly. "Do you think they saw us coming out of Father Lou's?"

"I think so," Ophelia said."Cato said he didn't want to alert the priest across the way, so he must have seen."

"It's still safer than the attic," Linus said.

"Then let's get him over to Father Lou as soon as the sun is up," Walter said.

"Shouldn't we do it now?" asked Linus.

Walter shook his head. "Quasi doesn't seem to be the kind of person I'd want to wake out of a dead sleep."

He doesn't seem to be the kind of person who goes into a dead sleep at all, thought Linus. But he held his tongue. He didn't realize it then, of course, but had he spoken up, it might have made all the difference. He should have listened to his newfound intuition.

Naturally, the morning's events failed to go exactly as planned.

Uncle Augustus had arisen early, made it to the hardware store by 8:00 a.m., and then enlisted the help of his niece and nephew by 8:30. As they were sitting around the breakfast table, he announced his horrible plans for the day. Dusty, dirty, filthy, disgusting plans.

Uncle Augustus buttered his toast bite-by-bite, while expounding (stating in detail) how to properly rip up carpet—the carpet in the living room, to be precise.

It was terrible carpet, to be sure. It should have been ripped up when Auggie and Portia moved into the building two decades before. Why anybody thought vines and frogs—disgusting dirty, slimy frogs—seemed a delightful motif (a repeated form in a design) for persons to walk across remains a mystery to this day. Thankfully, it is no more.

"So after you've removed all of the furniture, you'll pull up the carpet from the nail strips around the edges of the room. Then take those utility knives"—he pointed to a paper bag sitting on the counter—"and cut the carpet into four-foot wide strips. Roll up the strips and secure them with duct tape, a roll of which can be found, for your convenience, in that same bag. And wear those face masks while you're working, please. Who knows what's lurking in all of that dust and dirt?"

I find I cannot even think about that right now. Moving right along . . .

At 11:11 a.m., even with Walter's help, and with only twenty-four hours left in Quasimodo's visit, the twins were still slaving away. Now they were prying up the nail strips with a flathead screwdriver and a hammer. Linus found that part to be quite satisfying.

Ophelia grumbled, "There's no telling what Cato and Frollo will do. We've got to think of something."

Linus knew this to be true. Heavens, but he knew. Besides, she'd already muttered the exact same thing at least twenty times that morning. And poor Quasi was upstairs in the attic by himself. At least they'd managed to sneak up some cold cereal and a bottle of milk.

When he took a bite of the sugary cereal that Aunt Portia wasn't savvy (worldly wise) enough to know not to buy for teenagers, a look of amazement crossed his face. "This is delicious!"

"I know!" said Ophelia, who also loves sweets. Right then she realized she would put together a backpack of goodies to send home with him—a care package, if you will. She figured if objects from Book World could make the trip into Real World, then it stood to reason that the opposite was also true.

Finally, around noon, they'd stripped the living room floor bare. Uncle Augustus sidled into the room to have a look. "Well done! Take the rest of the day off."

They all sat back on their heels and sighed in relief.

"Oh, and the town's engineers think the dam is going to hold just fine. Good news that, eh? Take a look outside!"

Linus pulled back the curtain to reveal not exactly a sunny day, but the rain had finally stopped.

"See you later, Uncle Auggie," Ophelia said as she hurried from the room.

"Nothing like a clear in the weather to raise your spirits!" Uncle Augustus cried to their backs.

Walter headed over to Kingscross School to shower and change clothes. Meanwhile, the twins hurried up the steps to the attic, only to find that Quasimodo was gone!

"Cato knew I was awake!" Ophelia fumed. She'd been duped, deceived, and felt more gullible than the nerdy girl who's suddenly taken under the wing of the cool group in one of those awful teen movies.

She did not care for this feeling one bit.

Clearly, I was happy not to be Cato Grubbs at that particular point in time. You would have been as well.

sixteen

Sometimes Fourteen Years Is Plenty of Time to Accumulate the Necessary Brain Function to Figure Out How to Proceed

Linus fetched Walter as Ophelia, still angry but trying her best to remain calm, searched the room for a clue as to where the other, and obviously new and improved, enchanted circle might be found. Surely Cato would take their friend there. She hoped they could get to Quasi before it was too late. Quasi simply couldn't go back to Book World under those circumstances—right back into the stocks. It would be too cruel!

Ophelia looked under and around the scientific equipment, on the bookshelves, and then finally began rummaging through an old dresser. Just then, the little wooden carving of the dove came to life. At this point Ophelia wasn't surprised, but she was certainly surprised that she wasn't surprised! The dove alighted on a shoebox full of receipts that sat tucked in the top dresser drawer, then flew away to sit on the edge of an empty beaker.

Well, whatever, thought Ophelia as she began searching through the box.

Most of the receipts were from the hardware store or the grocery store, the usual electronically printed curls of paper. One, however, was a handwritten receipt from a shoe repair shop: Clean up and re-stitch red spangled party shoes—twenty dollars.

Cato stole Dorothy's ruby slippers! Ophelia couldn't believe it; but then again, yes she could. If she could travel into a book, she'd definitely abscond (steal and run) with those shoes. She might even try to bring back that little picnic basket in which to carry the little dog she hoped to own one day. (No dog yet, by the way. Aunt Portia is severely allergic.)

According to the address on the receipt, the shoe repair shop was located about three blocks away, not far from that street where college students go to drink coffee and feel—what do they say now?—hip.

Ophelia went downstairs and showed the receipt to the boys. She said, "It isn't much to go on, but at least it's something."

In ten minutes time, the three stood before Mr. Pine's Shoe Repair, 56 Scout Alley. An old brass bell clanged against the door as they entered, and a man looked up from the worktable at the back of the shop. He pulled off his half eyes (reading glasses that rest on the end, not the bridge, of the nose) and squinted at them. His pale blue eyes reminded Linus of a Siberian Husky. And his facial hair, dark sideburns leading into a white beard, helped the overall sled dog image as well. The man quickly stood to his feet—he was Ophelia's height.

"Can I help you?"

"Are you Mr. Pine?" asked Ophelia.

"No. Mr. Pine was the original owner. I bought the place several years ago and just kept the name. I'm Jack."

"We're trying to find the man who brought these shoes to you." She handed Jack the receipt. "He used to live where we live now. Yesterday we brought up a bunch of stuff from our basement—just in case it flooded—and a lot of the stuff is his."

Nicely done, Ophelia! Not a lie to be found. Of course, her stated intent was hardly on the up and up, so you must decide whether or not what she did was wrong. I'm not one to make that kind of judgment in a situation so dire. They simply had to find Quasimodo, you see, because less than twenty-four hours remained for him to get back inside the enchanted circle or end up like the Wicked Witch of the West.

Now there's someone that nobody wants to see come through the circle.

No one knew if a character could enter Real World in one circle and leave it through another. Not Ophelia, at least, and she certainly wouldn't take that chance with somebody as nice as Quasimodo. Besides, if she put him back in Book World, she'd do so at a time that would implicate Frollo as a witch, and then Quasi would be free to live the sort of life he deserved.

"I definitely remember him," Jack said. "Let me look him up in the book I use to keep track of my customers' info—just in case they don't show up to get their shoes." He reached under the counter and pulled out an old composition book (the black and white speckled notebook you most likely used in school when learning how to form letters).

"Don't you have a computer?" Linus asked.

"Yes, of course I have a computer," Jack said in a mocking voice. "I just prefer not to use it for the really important stuff. Now, let's see ..." Jack ran a finger down one page, flipped it to the next one, and then finally the next. "Here it is. Cato Grubbs. 461 Bovary."

Ophelia leaned over to look at the page. "Oh look! That is him!"

Next to each entry, Jack had drawn a tiny cartoon portrait of the customer. "I'm a bit of an amateur cartoonist." He blushed.

"Nicely done!" said Walter.

"Do you recognize that street name, Ophelia?" asked Linus. "I don't."

"I've never been there," Ophelia said.

"It's close by," said Jack. "Just take a right onto Heathcliff Street at the corner there, go one block, and then turn right onto Bovary."

"Thanks," she said. "We'd better get a move on. Nice meeting you."

"Anytime." He pushed a bowl of peppermint candies forward, and they each took one unwrapping the cellophane as they exited the shop.

Walter shoved the candy to the side of his mouth and placed his hands in the front pockets of his shorts as they set off down the sidewalk. "So off to Bovary, then. I wonder if the new enchanted circle is there?"

They walked up the hipster street lined with one bike shop, two vintage clothing boutiques, three bars offering live music every night, and four coffee shops. Oh, and I'm forgetting the CD exchange store.

Kingscross really is a lovely town, with flowers and trees growing all over the place. Some of the streets are still paved in brick, such as the one the threesome traversed (moved over) now. Heathcliff Street, the center of the good goings-on, ribboned across the highest point in town. And one important detail to know right now is that Rickshaw Street (where Seven Hills Better Books sits) is at the lowest point in town where the Bard River runs through it. So it was a bit of a climb to find Cato Grubbs.

Doing the things that one has to do for the sake of the greater good usually involves a climb of some sort. Get used to it. Life is not easy. There is room for only so many talentless pop stars and reality TV nincompoops, believe it or not, and thank goodness for that. The rest of us have to rise by the sweat of our own brow.

Walter chewed up the candy and then swallowed. "So, here we go then. What about a game plan, mates? Truly you're not thinking we'll simply pop on over, knock on the door, and say, 'Hello there, Mr. Grubbs. We've come to take back our hunchback.'"

"Not hardly," Ophelia chuckled. "We do need a plan though. The good thing is they probably don't know what we look—wait. Cato saw me lying on the sofa this morning. Drat."

"Walter's our best bet." Linus pointed at the street sign for the next intersection. "Bovary."

"Right, then." Walter stopped. "Let's think about this. You two probably shouldn't walk down the street with me. And I'll have to knock on the door under false pretenses. What should I say?"

Ophelia looked up, clearly thinking. "It can't be that you're selling something to raise money for school. First off, it's summer vacation; and second, they might just slam the door in your face."

Linus thought about the door-to-door sales he used to do back in Arizona to raise money for a band trip. He shuddered. Who wants a bunch of wrapping paper and candles? Now candy bars or popcorn, those he could work his mind around! And can't we all?

"Keep it simple," Linus said. "You're lost and need directions."

"Yes! And your accent will be perfect, Walter!" Ophelia added.

"Right." Walter inhaled deeply. "Just keep watch from up the street in case something goes wrong."

seventeen

Don't Ever Underestimate the Brilliance of Street Smarts

*W*alter and worry rarely mixed. In London, Walter was what people back in my day called a "juvenile delinquent" (what's known today as a "troubled teen"). In other words, sometimes he got into things that he really should have avoided. The police (or "bobbies" as they call them over there) delivered Walter to his mum's doorstep from time to time, and they even tried to frighten him with a night in jail.

No wonder Auntie Max offered him a year at Kingscross School.

But Walter wasn't stupid—or evil. He was undeniably bored and just seemed to fall in with people who were always looking for trouble. Kingscross was to be his fresh start, so what he used to do in the past is none of our business. He was as ready for a clean slate as anyone else would be. Looking over your shoulder becomes tiresome after a while.

Therefore, knocking on somebody's door and asking for directions was less than nothing, perhaps a negative fifteen, to a young man like Walter.

The houses on Bovary stood shoulder to shoulder and shared the sidewalls. Some people call such dwellings "rowhouses." Not at all large, they were gathered together in a humbler section of town than where the Kingscross School stood. Yet each owner lovingly cared for their property by painting the façades (front outside walls) a variety of cheerful hues. And all of the homes were friendly and welcoming, festooned with wreathes and other seasonal decorations such as birdhouses and cinnamon brooms. Except, naturally, the house in front of Walter.

Cato's neighbors must really be chapped, Walter thought as he compared the peeling, sickly green coat of paint on the house in front of him to the sunflower gold on his right and the Caribbean blue on his left.

Walter rapped on the door and waited.

He rapped again.

"Hold your pants on! I'm coming!" a gravelly female voice yelled.

When the door opened, Walter's intuition kicked in. Say what you will about kids with street smarts, but sometimes it comes in handy.

"I'm looking for Cato Grubbs," he said with confidence.

"That bum!" the woman squinted at him, her beady eyes practically disappearing into a rather large face framed by long straight hair that was blacker than black. "He doesn't live here anymore. You're not related to him, are you?"

Walter sighed. "Wouldn't you know it? And somehow I got the job of informing him about some family matters." He leaned forward as if to share a secret with her, "I'm only fourteen, yet I'm the sanest one in the bunch, I can tell you that."

She leaned against the doorframe and said, "That doesn't surprise me. He was sure an odd one. Hardly ever here. Almost every night around ten o'clock, he'd head out the door with a big satchel over his shoulder or a box of junk under his arm." She pointed in the direction from which Walter had just come. "And he always went thataway."

Back to his lab, thought Walter.

"So I take it he no longer lives here?"

"Kicked him out."

"Was he your—" Walter leaned forward again and turned on the charm "—boyfriend?"

She laughed and, despite her distrustful appearance, the sound was pleasant and clear.

Maybe she just needs to laugh more, thought Walter.

"Definitely not! He was just a boarder here. And he was three months behind on his rent, too."

"Was there, perhaps, a circle painted on the floor of his bedroom?"

"How did you—"

"Family crest," Walter said quickly. Please, dear God, let her believe that miserable explanation.

"Ah," she nodded, "you're English."

"Yes, ma'am. I am. Right, then. Well, thank you very much, Miss ..." Walter held out his hand.

She took it and gave it a shake. "Fanny. Just call me Fanny."

"Thanks again ever so much, Fanny," he said with a courtly little bow. He hoped she might think: *It's a shame more young people aren't like him nowadays. If they were, I'd have hope for the future.*

"He's moved, but she said he used to come this way every night," Walter told Linus and Ophelia once he'd rejoined them.

"So enchanted circle number two clearly wasn't there," said Ophelia.

"Yes, it was. But apparently if he can make a second circle, then he can make a third one as well."

"Improving upon the design as he goes," said Linus. The man's a genius. And mad. But he's a genius still.

They headed back toward the bookshop.

"What do we do now?" asked Ophelia.

Walter stopped to scratch his ankle. "We go get a decent cup of tea and put on our thinking caps. Maybe Father Lou will help us. He used to be involved with a rather unsavory segment of society."

"And Cato Grubbs certainly fits that description," said Ophelia, remembering his plan to steal Esmeralda's necklace. She didn't like Esmeralda, but the Gypsy woman didn't deserve to have her only prized possession snatched from around her neck. But that tambourine she danced around with was another matter.

Ophelia hated folk songs.

eighteen

Why Does It Seem Like a Crime
to Stop for a Bite of Lunch?

The Bard River was running high, no doubt about it. If it rose another foot, the basement of All Souls, as well as the first floor of the manse, would be a muddy mess when the waters finally abated (decreased).

The riverbank could be seen from Father Lou's kitchen, where they all sat wondering about their friend Quasimodo. Father Lou set the teapot and mugs on the kitchen table and told the young people to help themselves.

"So you've lost Quasi," he said.

"Yes!" Ophelia heard herself wail. She hated it when people talked like that. "It's horrible," she said more calmly. "And we have only—" she looked at the kitchen clock, "twenty-one hours left to find him."

"Does he know what will happen to him if he doesn't get back to the circle on time?"

The three shook their heads simultaneously. Ophelia shuddered and explained. It was terrible to even think of it, let alone talk about it.

Father Lou tightened the band on his white ponytail. "In my experience with finding the more unsavory elements of society, people don't usually move up when they get kicked out of a place. So don't look for Cato in a nicer neighborhood. You're going to have to go over to the east end of town. And I'm going with you. Let me go change clothes first."

"Wow," whispered Ophelia, "Is it that rough over there? Oh, man."

Excitement tripped along Walter's nerves.

Tea is fine, thought Linus, *but are we ever going to grab some lunch? It's two o'clock!*

They stepped outside.

"No rain," said Ophelia. "Hopefully the dam will hold."

"It's still raining further upriver, so don't let this beautiful day fool you," warned Father Lou, now dressed in biker boots, jeans, and an old blue T-shirt.

Walter took out a pack of gum and offered a piece to everyone.

"It just depends on how old the dam is," said Linus, who knew all too well how so many of the structures that we take for granted are in desperate need of repair. I shall forego the details or you might never get in a car again.

Father Lou pointed beyond Paris Park and said, "The worst part of all this is that the place most likely to be destroyed by a flood is that summer camp on the other side of the park."

Linus knew of it — a camp for disabled and terminally ill children. If a flash flood came through and whisked away those kids, the level of tragedy would be higher than most people could bear to think about.

"Has anybody warned them?" Linus asked.

"Not that I know of. Let's go there first."

They turned right and headed up Rickshaw Street.

Walter picked up a stick and flipped it end over end, catching it as he walked along. "Most likely the dam won't burst. If we weren't worried about it then, yes, it most certainly would."

Father Lou laughed. "It will or it won't, Walter. I doubt our attitude has anything to do with it."

"I don't know," Linus said. "The only reason Chuck Yeager broke the sound barrier was because he was the first pilot who really thought he could do it. There was nothing different about the plane he used or anything."

Ophelia looked at her brother in surprise. "That's more words than you usually say in an entire day."

"I'm hungry," Linus changed the subject.

"We'll get some lunch after we find Quasi," she said.

Exactly what Linus didn't want to hear.

The Bard River Camp for Kids had been in operation since 1933. A collection of dark brown wooden buildings, the camp was spread out on about three acres of land. Shade trees stood around the cabins and the lodge. A swimming pool glistened in the sunlight.

As Father Lou and the three teens walked into the lodge, across the room they saw a wall of windows overlooking the rushing river. Several children rolled by them in their wheelchairs, others wore leg braces; some sported bald heads—an unfortunate result of their cancer treatments. In short, they all faced challenges that most of us do not. Yet the volume of their laughter disguised the seriousness of their conditions.

A young man looked up from where he sat playing a board game with three children. He walked over and introduced himself, "I'm Eric, the camp director. Can I help you folks?"

Father Lou asked if he knew about the dam.

Eric, eager and obviously good with kids since he seemed like a big kid himself, nodded. "Yes, we heard about it. But the weatherman says the rain has stopped for good, so I think we'll be all right. I appreciate you coming by, though."

"All right, then," said Father Lou, handing the young man his business card. "Call me if you need anything or, God forbid—"

"Mr. Eric!" a child called from a nearby table where several girls were doing a craft.

"Thanks for coming by," said Eric. "Gotta go."

As they walked down the drive, Walter commented, "Eric didn't seem too worried."

"Does the camp have an evacuation plan?" asked Ophelia.

"I don't know," said Father Lou, "but at least we tried."

Twenty minutes later they stood in the middle of the infamous (famous for being bad) east end of town. Linus gazed around, wondering what the neighborhood looked like when freshly built homes waited to be inhabited and people held a little more hope in their hearts. Most of the homes were single-story ones with small yards surrounded by chain-link fences that sagged with age. And apparently only a few people had ever heard of a lawn mower.

At least a third of the houses were boarded up, and it seemed ten degrees hotter over here.

Somebody was grilling close-by. As Linus inhaled the delicious aroma, his stomach growled. He felt a little guilty that right now he'd rather find a hamburger than Quasi.

Ophelia pulled out the old photograph of Cato and handed it to Father Lou. "This is the only picture we have of him."

He examined it. "That's some fancy dude right there."

"That's good," said Ophelia. "He'll be easily recognizable to people."

Walter snorted at her optimism.

Father Lou laughed and turned to him, "Exactly, Walter."

"Huh?" asked Linus.

"No matter how distinct Cato Grubbs looks, people in this part of town won't be willing to say much."

"Precisely," said Walter.

Ophelia sighed. "I guess we have a lot to learn about this stuff."

"Seems so." Father Lou looked up and down the street and then pointed to a steeple. "But here's where we have the advantage: Mutual respect of the clergy. Let's go."

Now Walter might have chuckled at the twins' obvious cluelessness about the less-than-savory element of society, but he was a touch envious that they'd never have to know the things that he did.

The steeple grew from the roof of a small church called East End Assemblies of God.

"This should be interesting," said Father Lou. "These folks are a heck of lot less reserved than we Episcopalians are."

Linus wanted to laugh at that mental image. *Yeah, Father Lou's problem is his shyness and his tendency to clam up around people*, Linus thought.

Soon enough, the church secretary showed them into Pastor Bob Campbell's office. Pastor Bob stood at Linus's height, had perfectly combed hair, and wore a well-cut suit. To be truthful, he looked like a stockbroker. The pastors introduced themselves and joked about how, judging by their clothing, they should probably switch churches.

Father Lou pulled out the photo of Cato. "We're looking for

someone. And I won't lie to you, Bob, he's not a nice person. But we need to find him. He's believed to be with someone very important to us, and let's just say his intent toward our friend isn't good."

Pastor Bob raised his eyebrows. "Oh my! Well, let's have a look."

Father Lou placed the photo in Bob's hand.

"Oh my!" Bob said again.

"Do you know where he is?" asked Ophelia hopefully.

"No. But that suit sure is ridiculous!"

"Drat," Ophelia said. "We were hoping you'd know him."

"I moved here just a couple of weeks ago," he said as he turned toward the office door. "Molly! Can you come in here for a second?"

The middle-aged secretary returned to the pastor's office. She had tomato-red hair, and she was wearing a pair of tight jeans and a shirt she must have purchased when her midsection wasn't quite so apparent (exposed).

Bob handed Molly the picture and asked, "Have you ever seen this guy?"

She handed it right back to him. "Yeah, just a couple of hours ago. He was in Fischer's Market down the street buying a jar of mayo and some cans of tuna. I was behind him in the checkout line."

"Do you know where he lives?" Ophelia asked.

"Not exactly. But I think he might be on Crane Street. I've seen him round that corner a few times."

"Thank you," said Father Lou. "We appreciate the help."

"Anytime," Pastor Bob said with an easy wave as Molly shot him a look of disbelief. "Always here to lend a hand."

Back out on the sidewalk, Father Lou turned to his three companions. "Man, that guy has a lot to learn about this neighborhood."

"Molly will make sure he does," said Walter.

Father Lou retucked his T-shirt into the waistband of his jeans. "Well? Shall we keep hoofing it?"

"Absolutely," Walter said.

"Of course!" Ophelia was getting into the spirit of things now.

Great, thought Linus. *Could we at least stop someplace so I can buy a candy bar?*

nineteen

What Does It Take for a Guy to Get Some Lunch Around Here?

𝒜pparently the candy bar would have to wait.

"That's the place." Ophelia pointed to a narrow, one-story shack, where the rooms appear to be lined up single file. In some places this type of home is called a "shotgun shack" due to the fact that you could shoot a gun inside the front door and the ammunition would go clear through the house and right out the back door—provided that door was standing open. If not, then I suppose a new back door would be in order, wouldn't it?

"Cato seems to leave peeling paint behind him wherever he goes," Walter commented as he reached out and picked off a large flake of pink paint with his fingernail. "How do we know this is it?"

"That." Ophelia pointed toward a windowsill where a Roman dagger sat in plain sight. "It looks just like the one we found in the basement."

Walter scratched an itch on the back of his head. "I don't know why, but I figured you could bring something back with you from Book World just once. Or can you go in again with a different copy of the same book?"

Ophelia shrugged. "Maybe you get another chance with a different enchanted circle."

"Or maybe it's some other Roman's dagger," Linus snapped. "Can we get on with this?"

"Well, aren't we testy?" said Ophelia.

"Have at it." Father Lou motioned toward the front door.

Walter stepped forward. "I'll do it."

The hair on the back of Walter's neck stood up like a porcupine's quills. Approaching a strange house on Bovary was one thing, but here? He knew a rough part of town when he saw it. After all, he'd just moved away from the rough part of town back home.

Walter knocked on the mud-colored door (he didn't like this house one bit) and waited. He knocked again. Still nothing. He shrugged in the direction of the others who were waiting on the sidewalk two doors down.

Right, then. I didn't think I'd need this skill anymore, but apparently I was wrong. Walter reached for his wallet in the back pocket of his shorts, and pulled out a lock pick. He could just imagine the look of surprise on Father Lou's face—not that the priest would be too surprised. Walter figured rightly that Father Lou had been much like him in his youth.

Sliding the pick into the keyhole, he felt around in the mechanism to release the pins. He'd picked locks far more complicated than this one. The door was opened in less than three seconds.

Father Lou was already behind him. "Nice work, Walter."

"I'd rather not go into it."

"Smart guy. Let's see what we can find in here." Father Lou turned to the twins and said, "Linus, stay by the door in case they come running out. Ophelia, you be the lookout up and down the street."

This assignment was just fine with Ophelia. *Let the guys handle the dirty work*, she thought. Besides, her vision was definitely more keen than Linus's because he refused to wear his glasses.

"If you find that jar of mayonnaise and a can of tuna, bring it to me," Linus joked.

Walter stepped forward into the dark recesses of the house. Heavy gray curtains covered all the windows, dragging down rods that could barely support them. Had the drapes been open, one would have seen a wall of swirling dust in the sunbeams. Goodness. The squalor some people live in. The place needed more than just a good cleaning, that I know. One might consider calling in a hazmat (hazardous materials) team. And if that didn't work, then a total gutting of the interior would have been in order.

They trod softly through the living room that held just a card table, two folding chairs, and lots of cardboard boxes. A layer of brown dust—at least a quarter inch thick—covered everything. Continuing on down the hall toward the back of the house, they discovered the kitchen was in even worse shape than the living room. I can barely bring myself to describe the scene to you without my gag reflex kicking in. But a writer always serves the story—even at great personal cost. If you aren't willing to do that, then you might consider employment as a night watchman at a funeral home. The people you work with there should give you no trouble whatsoever.

At any rate, no dish had been washed in months. Once painted an eager yellow, the kitchen walls were now glazed with a greasy brown haze. Having apparently used up all of the good china, Cato had switched to paper plates and plastic cutlery. These items now littered every inch of horizontal space in the room, save for a narrow pathway on the floor.

I cannot talk about the bugs, however. I leave it up to you to use your imagination. Thank you.

Walter did what I would do, what you would do, what almost anyone without a terrible head cold or who works as a medical examiner or sewer employee would do—he held his hand up to his mouth, turned away, and tried not to regurgitate (throw up).

Lou clapped Walter on the back while holding his own nose, but he looked completely at home despite the odor. "If the circle is in here, he hasn't used it in weeks. Let's try the bedrooms."

Walter nodded gratefully, now reticent (unsure) about searching the rest of the house at all. Who knew what the bathroom would be like?

I'd rather not think about that either.

The first bedroom, directly behind the kitchen, sat empty except for a couple of suitcases filled with Cato's showy clothing, and a blanket and pillow tossed onto the stained carpet that may have once looked like a summer sky. The bathroom door was closed, thank goodness. But they didn't need to see what was in there anyway, because when they opened the door to the second bedroom, there sat Quasimodo. He was gagged with a handkerchief

and tied up like a fly trapped in a spider's web. Still, he was trying his best to work loose the cords.

"Quasi!" Father Lou knelt beside Quasimodo and pulled the gag from his mouth.

"You all right, mate?" asked Walter as he took out a large pen-knife. This, of course, gave Father Lou no cause for surprise.

"Uh-huh," said Quasi, puckering and unpuckering his lips.

Walter began cutting the ropes. He slipped the blade under a strand, and then with a quick, decisive one-two slide of the blade, the cord popped apart. One more cut farther down, and both Father Lou and Walter worked the ropes free.

"They knocked me over the head," Quasi said. "Otherwise, they never would have taken me."

All males have their pride, you know, even hunchbacks from the Middle Ages.

"I believe it," said Walter. "Those two don't equal one of you in strength."

Despite his upbringing, Walter knew exactly what to say to encourage someone who was feeling less than his best.

Father Lou held out a hand and pulled Quasi to his feet. "Let's get you out of this house, and then we'll figure out how to get you back to Rickshaw Street. You might be a little conspicuous (easily noticed) in broad daylight."

Linus and Ophelia hurried in once they got the all clear. Ophelia hugged Quasimodo close. "I'm so glad you're safe," she whispered in his ear.

"Where did Cato and Frollo get off to?" Walter asked.

"They left a few minutes ago to get something to eat," Quasimodo said while rubbing his sore wrists.

Figures, thought Linus.

twenty

No Sense in Sitting Around All Day, Trust Me

*f*ather Lou treated them all to a hot dog from the lunch cart on Havisham and Rickshaw. Linus had given Quasimodo his ball cap, which made him a tad less noticeable. But if someone did happen to notice Quasi, the stares—some horrified, some mocking, some filled with pity—shot through them all. Except for Quasi.

He failed to notice anything as he took in his surroundings in wonder. Cars especially pleased him. "No horses? No oxen? No donkeys? Amazing!"

"Freak!" someone yelled out the window of a passing van.

"There's that word again," said Quasimodo. "What's a 'freak'?"

"Someone who's more special than most people," said Father Lou.

"I hear what you're saying, Father." Quasi smiled. "But back in Paris, I'm called an animal, grotesque, and an abomination. 'Freak' sounds much better than those things."

Talk about looking on the bright side, thought Linus.

Ophelia, aching for her new friend, took her hot dog from the vendor. "Thanks, Father Lou. But I have to eat and run. I've got to finish reading that book by tomorrow morning, and I've still got a ways to go."

The four guys watched her take off down the street.

"I hope she reads fast," Quasimodo said as he took a bite of his hot dog. "This is delicious! Food tastes so much better here."

Walter gave him a friendly slap on the back, which was really a slap on the hump. "Too bad you can't stay."

"I know," Quasi whispered, and then he sat down on a bench next to Father Lou.

Linus said nothing as he remained at the hot dog cart, piling as much sauerkraut, pickle relish, onions, and mustard onto his hot dog as he could.

Quasi was back. Lunch was finally served. Life was good.

But not for long.

As Linus finished the final bite of his hot dog, that same group of touch football players whom Quasi and Walter had encountered in the park the day before came striding through the park gates.

"Hey!" shouted Brian, their leader, "I thought I told you not to bring that loser around here anymore."

Walter stood ready to fight. He'd gotten into fights after much less provocation (something that irritates or angers) than this fellow! "You said nothing of the sort. Of course, I don't suppose someone with a brain like yours can remember back that far."

Uh-oh, thought Linus, quickly remembering all the fights he'd been in—which was zero. Did you punch with the eye of your fist face up or with your knuckles?

The gang advanced on them rapidly. Brian swung a wild punch at Walter who simply grabbed his wrist and then pulled and pivoted, sending the lad facedown into a muddy puddle on the street.

"Nicely done!" shouted Father Lou.

Brian scrambled to his feet. "Well?" he shouted to his crew. "What are you all standing around for?"

Of course, Brian couldn't see himself just then, what with his face all scraped and muddy, and his clothes a wreck.

The largest boy on their team shook his head. "You're on your own, man. You've gone too far making fun of that guy."

"Yeah," said the next largest, wiping the sweat off his brow with the hem of his orange T-shirt. "This is bogus."

"What does 'bogus' mean?" whispered Quasi.

The young men turned their backs on their former leader and headed off down the street. Now abandoned by his mates, Brian turned and slunk off in the opposite direction.

"Wow, Walter!" said Father Lou. "Great move. Very tai chi."

"I just make sure I get out of the way," Walter said with a laugh.

Linus breathed a sigh of relief. Maybe he could get Walter to teach him a thing or two.

"I suppose we'll have to wait out Quasi's remaining hours in the attic," said Walter. "Just to be sure."

Linus wasn't having any of it, as his loquacious (long-winded, chatty) speech attested, "Quasi can't spend his last day in Real World cooped up in some attic."

"Come on over to the manse," Father Lou suggested.

"No. We need to show Quasi a good time," Linus insisted.

"You're right," Walter nodded as they set off down the street. "Look what he has to go back to. And besides, if we stay on the move, then Cato and Frollo will be far less likely to find us."

Father Lou had to admit that Walter had a good point. "Suit yourself. Where are you going now?"

"The park would be a good start," said Walter.

Oh great, thought Linus.

"Let's see how high the river is. Are you lads up for that?"

"Sure," said Linus. Whatever will be, will be.

"I guess I'll head home to write my sermon then," Father Lou said. "You know where I am if you need me. Please come by the manse later and let me know how things are going." Father Lou ambled down Rickshaw Street without them, rubbing the wooden cross on his necklace as he went.

Walter shoved his hands into his pockets and nodded his head toward the gates of Paris Park across the street. "Shall we?"

Linus stepped off the curb.

For the first time, Quasi experienced what it felt like to be in a group of guys, just hanging out and having a good time. He grinned so widely that Walter thought his face might split. It was the most gruesomely beautiful sight he'd ever seen.

Man, thought Linus. *That river looks like it's rolling by at fifty miles an hour.*

"I don't know what this river normally looks like," said Walter, "but it sure looks high to me."

Quasimodo said, "I hope the dam doesn't burst."

They sat at a wooden picnic table underneath the pavilion near the Bard River. Three more inches and the river would have covered their feet.

Linus had run down to the corner grocery store and procured

(gotten) all manner of snack food that Quasimodo would never get to eat again, but would probably remember with great relish. (In this case relish means "excitement," not the pickle condiment that Linus recently shoveled onto his hot dog.) Potato chips, pretzels, tortilla chips and salsa, cheese dip, chocolate bars, soda, and all manner of food that will rot one's body from the inside out.

Quasimodo enjoyed every bite, and mind you, he ate more bites than anybody else did. Linus could tell Quasi was trying hard not to bring down the mood; he forced a smile whenever Walter cracked a joke and even managed to laugh a time or two. But the fact sat with both boys that their new friend was headed back to a terrible life of social deprivation, boredom, and no central air. Not to mention the fact that he still loved Esmeralda.

Walter brought up the topic of the Gypsy girl after they'd opened the bag of party mix — "extra bold" flavor. "You've got to let her go, mate. She'll be your undoing."

"Love has a mind of its own," Quasi said as he reached into the bag, pulled out a melba toast round (pumpernickel flavor), and examined both sides before popping it into his mouth.

"Maybe," said Linus. "But it doesn't have to."

"He's right." Walter reached for the bag. "Sometimes a chap has to make a decision with his head, not his heart."

"She's just so beautiful," said Quasi.

"Of course," Linus said, thinking about Clarice Yardly-Poutsmouth's great beauty. And her great appetite. "Be smart, that's all we're saying."

All we can do is plant seeds, he thought. *Hopefully, Quasi will figure it out on his end when he returns home.*

Just then Eric and a group of kids from the camp next door appeared on the paved path beside the river. Their laughter and chatter filled the gaps between the young men, and the guys couldn't help but smile.

As they passed by the pavilion, the kids stopped. They were always ready to talk to anybody. Attending camp gave them that confidence — a lovely thing, to be sure.

A little boy with white-blond hair gave a little wave from his wheelchair. "Hi! You were at the lodge a little while ago!" he announced.

Walter got right up. "How are you doing, mate? The name's Walter."

"I'm Kyle."

Walter turned to introduce the others. "That's Quasi over there, the big guy. And the tall one is Linus."

"Whoa!" said Kyle, his blue eyes growing rounder, "You look like a strong guy, Quasi!"

"He is." Walter motioned Quasimodo forward, but he looked like he was about to be shown the gallows (a wooden frame from which a person is hanged). "Show him, Quasi."

Quasimodo's face registered panic for just a moment, but then his expression changed to one that Walter had yet to see in any context other than food.

It was sheer amazement.

Kyle had offered his hand for Quasimodo to shake.

"He's not from around here, Kyle," explained Walter. "This is what we do here, Quasi."

Walter took Kyle's bony hand in his and gave it a gentle shake. Then Kyle held his hand out toward Quasimodo again. Quasi slowly offered his own bony hand to the boy; but his hand wasn't frail, it was large and quite able to crush Kyle's tiny one. Quasi held the little boy's hand with the utmost gentleness, and the boy beamed.

Linus had to bite back the emotions that threatened to bring tears to his eyes. This tiny gesture would do more to change Quasi's future than anything Ophelia had ever said or done, and much more than anything he and Walter had tried to offer Quasi that afternoon. Or so Linus hoped.

Soon the other children gathered around Quasimodo as well. He picked them up and spun them around, holding them up over his head. Well, those whose physical states would allow it.

But when Quasi hoisted Kyle over his shoulder and climbed the large oak tree nearby, any reservation that someone might have had toward the young man who looked so different from the rest of the world, vanished.

Well, except for the young camp director who now shouted in a panic, "Get back down here!"

Kyle called down from above, "Look at me, Eric! I can see the world! I can see the whole world from up here!"

Quasi smiled and laughed. "Yes, you can, Kyle. And so can I!"

twenty-one

A River Will Do Whatever
a River Wants to Do

*W*hile Aunt Portia and Uncle Augustus were out for dinner with Ronda and Mr. Birdwistell, Walter and the twins taught Quasimodo how to play Gin Rummy, Scrabble, and Chinese Checkers. He found himself to be a real whiz at playing the kids' video games as well (mostly older ones about that little Italian plumber whose name I can never remember). Hide-and-seek? He'd never played it! (Oh, the outrage!) But Quasi loved the challenge of finding hiding places that would totally conceal him and his bulk.

Quasimodo was beginning to realize that no one had to sit back and let life just happen to him; he could face it head on and try to beat it.

He thought, *Perhaps I might be able to change things when I get back to Paris. Maybe with enough thought and planning, courage and faith, I can make a life for myself that isn't tragic — one that's filled with hope and meaning for myself and for those around me. It has to be possible!* He thought this last part to himself over and over again as the hours that remained until 11:11 a.m. dwindled down.

Ophelia wondered if her brain might explode. They'd decided to stay up all night so as not to miss a single minute with Quasimodo. And who could blame them? He proved himself a chap of the first degree—not at all like some actors' portrayals of him in the movies. In fact, Walter slipped off to the video store to rent a copy of "The Hunchback of Notre Dame," the silent version from

1923 with Lon Chaney playing Quasimodo. (If you watch it some-time, you might get as big a kick out of it as I did.)

Linus made some popcorn, heavy on the butter and salt, and by 9:00 p.m. the four of them were sitting in Ophelia's room with their eyes glazed over, hands automatically traveling from bowls to mouths as the story played out before them. As soon as the actor jumped up on the balustrade of the Cathedral of Notre-Dame and started jeering at the people and sticking out his tongue at those gathered below, Quasimodo jerked his head back with a start. "That's how I'm perceived?" he asked.

"That's just the actor's interpretation," Ophelia said. "It couldn't be further from the truth though, could it?"

"Why would I do that?" Quasi set down his popcorn bowl. "What did any of them ever do to me? I just hang around the Cathe-dral. And you know what? People appreciate how I ring the bells. They know I do that for them. I do it to bring happiness to people."

It was clear he was getting flustered.

"It's just a movie," Linus said.

They'd already explained to Quasimodo what a movie was before they started the DVD player. Not easy.

Walter chimed in, "It's not a personal attack on you, Quasi. Before the past couple of days, you were just someone created in the mind of a novelist a long time ago. Only we three and Father Lou know you as a real person."

"And you're very, very real!" said Ophelia, patting him on the shoulder. She gestured toward the TV screen, "Just look at this for the funny thing that it is."

"I'll try," he said with a sigh.

Ophelia stole glances at Quasi during the rest of the film. She realized that watching the tragic tale of the hunchback being acted out on the screen was doing more to help him than anything they could have said to him. He watched as Esmeralda fell more and more hopelessly in love with Captain Phoebus, the handsome mili-tary man who would only use her affection. He watched as Frollo, still fraught with love for Esmeralda, cast all caution and wisdom to the devil in order to obtain her. And most of all, he watched himself, caught in the middle as an unwitting player, innocent and gullible in the workings of those who were willing to do anything to get what they wanted or thought they needed.

He drew in a shaky breath. "Oh, I don't think I can take any more of this. Maybe I should go back up to the attic."

Linus immediately turned off the DVD player.

"We wouldn't think of it, Quasi," said Walter.

Quasi seemed as if he were in a dream; he shook his head. "Do you think there's a fate for someone like me, a person created in someone else's mind? Do I have a will of my own somehow, now that ... well, now that I'm here and I'm real—" he slapped himself on the forearm "—flesh and blood? Or am I doomed to live out what Victor Hugo decided for me long ago?"

They all stared at him in sorrow. Nobody knew the answer to that question—nobody, of course, except Cato Grubbs. And thankfully, he wasn't around to tell them the answer.

At 4:30 a.m., Walter looked out the window and across the street. By now they'd played enough games to last them a month. "The kitchen light is on at the manse. We should go see what Father Lou is up to."

Everyone agreed.

As they crossed Rickshaw Street, Walter said, "I could really do with a proper cup of tea."

"So could I," said Quasi who admitted it was his favorite beverage since his crossover to Real World.

"I shouldn't be coming with you," Ophelia said as she stepped up onto the curb. "I still have a hundred pages left to read."

"Plenty of time," said Linus.

"I do read rather quickly," she said—not to boast, but to convince herself that this break would be all right in the end.

Honestly, I think she was rather irresponsible in taking a risk like that, what with the horrible prospect of Quasimodo fizzing down to nothing more than a pile of smoking rags. But nobody ever listens to me.

Father Lou opened the kitchen door right away and said, "I'm not surprised to see you all." He showed them in and turned to Quasimodo. "Not much time left, huh?"

"No, sir."

"Well, we'll certainly miss you," he said. "Sit down, everyone, and I'll get us some tea."

Ophelia pulled out a chair. "Walter was hoping you'd say that."

"Absolutely." Walter grinned as he sat down.

"What's that noise?" Quasimodo cocked an ear toward the sound of voices coming from what looked like a radio of some fashion.

"A police scanner." Father Lou spooned tea leaves into a brown teapot. "Old habits die hard. And it's the only thing worth listening to at this time of night." He filled the electric kettle with water and set it on its base to heat.

First, they chatted about incidentals (not terribly exciting matters), and then the kids helped Father Lou get caught up on all the happenings of the rest of their day. Just as Quasimodo began telling the priest how much he loved Scrabble and was planning to carve a set of his own wooden alphabet tiles upon his return, a bolt of lightning cut him off midsentence as it illuminated the thin white curtains at the window. A crack of thunder quickly followed, and then rain—torrents of rain—split the night sky, spilling down onto the church and into the already swollen Bard River.

They looked at one another.

"I hope ..." began Ophelia.

But she knew. They all felt the importance of the moment, remembering the instability of the dam.

Father Lou turned up the scanner. "If something happens to that dam, we'll hear about it on this. I'll make another pot of tea."

twenty-two

Where Two or Three Are Gathered Together, a Lot More Gets Done

The vigil began. A vigil means someone is keeping watch, usually at night, and that person will often stay awake into the wee hours of the morning. Nowadays people use that term for anything that happens after 7:00 p.m. and utilizes candles. Most of these events are actually memorial services or polite protests, but let's not spoil the meaning for them. It's the thought that counts, eh?

The gang was still sitting around Father Lou's kitchen table a while later. Before setting out the tea things, he'd covered the table with a lace tablecloth found in one of the kitchen drawers. It was in such opposition to his personality, yet somehow it was entirely fitting. The hands on the wall clock, which looked like a large pocket watch, seemed to speed around the face. It was almost 6:00 a.m. already. Only five hours left until Quasimodo's departure, and here they sat, listening to a police scanner and hoping against hope that bad news wouldn't be transmitted from speaker to eardrum.

"This situation might call for something a little stronger," said Father Lou as he rose from his chair, opened the refrigerator, and pulled out a bag of coffee.

Now you're talking, thought Linus. *Tea was okay but nothing more than that.*

A voice from the scanner said, "Engineers have judged the dam to be severely compromised. They say it may give way soon — probably in less than fifteen minutes, but maybe in as much as an hour. Hard to tell."

All of their spines stiffened at this news.

"The camp," Quasi gasped, a look of fear on his face.

"The entire street!" Walter jumped up from his chair. "Many people won't be awake at this time."

"We have to get those kids to higher ground," said Father Lou as he slipped on his boots that were sitting by the back door.

"Rickshaw Street needs to be evacuated as well," said Ophelia. The police scanner burbled. "It's not looking good here."

"Quasi! We can use the bells!" Father Lou shouted with excitement. "Head on up to the bell tower and ring them for all they're worth!"

"Yes, Father!" Quasimodo jumped from his chair and hurried out the door, looking surprisingly graceful as he did so.

"Ophelia. Wake your aunt and uncle and start knocking on doors to warn everyone. Linus. Walter. Let's get over to the camp right now!"

As they dispersed outside the manse, they looked up to see the shadowy figure of Quasimodo scaling the wall toward the window of the bell tower. Despite the rain, his fingers dug into the crevices between the stonework. His arm muscles constricted into strong cords, looking limber and lithe and as coordinated as a cat.

"The door was locked!" he called down to them. And a second later, he disappeared into the darkness behind the window.

As the storyteller, choosing whose viewpoint from which to tell the current scene can be an excruciating decision. The writer tries to pick the most compelling point of view, but sometimes, as is the case here, they're all quite compelling—all perspectives are of equal value, yet they're all very different from each other.

Quasimodo was utilizing a very different set of bells—ones not requiring his full weight. As such, with the first pull of the rope, he'd come crashing down onto his poor knees. Ophelia awakened her aunt and uncle, and then the three of them divided up Rickshaw Street, knocking on doors as loudly as they could and yelling, "The dam is about to burst! Get to higher ground! Get to higher ground!" (*And I feel compelled to add here that Aunt Portia's hair was a sight.*) The police arrived on the scene a full five minutes after Ophelia and her guardians had already begun warning people.

Linus, Walter, and Father Lou were taking great care with the children at the camp, most of whom weren't as frightened as one might think. This might have been due to the fact that they were plenty used to medical emergencies—sometimes riding in ambulances in the middle of the night—and almost constantly relying on other people to do the right thing by them.

Kyle chattered the entire time about how exciting it all was as Linus carried him toward the camp's minibus.

The camp director had gone pale.

"Is Quasi all right?" the little boy asked.

"He's fine." Linus set the boy down on a bus seat.

"I wish we could get more news about the dam," said Father Lou as he walked by carrying two six-year-olds, one on each hip.

Quasi's bells sounded in the background. He'd quickly composed a carillon (a tune played on a set of bells) that was jarring and ominous, yet somehow beautiful. It's amazing to discover the various talents people have—skills and abilities of which we might never have become aware. If someone didn't awaken to the sound of these bells, it was surely no fault of Quasi's.

By the time the last camper was in her seat and Eric started driving the minibus toward higher ground, the university's infirmary—where Father Lou had already called to make arrangements for the children to stay the night—was ready.

"We'll get to eat in the cafeteria tomorrow! Yeah!" shouted Kyle as the minibus pulled away. Father Lou followed them in the church van so he could help unload everyone.

Linus and Walter hurried back toward the church. They met Ophelia, Aunt Portia, and Uncle Augustus in front of the bookshop. People scurried about (most of them carrying one bag filled with precious heirlooms or, at the very least, a laptop computer) and headed toward Havisham, climbing the hill to reach higher ground. The rain pummeled (beat or thrashed) the earth so heavily that every single person looked as though they'd been dared to sit in the dunking booth at the town carnival, and the ball had struck its target every time.

Without warning, the bells ceased ringing. A terrible silence settled around them for several seconds, a thick silence that one feels more than hears because this silence doesn't denote (mark or signal) an ending—it says something awful has begun.

As suddenly as they'd ceased, the bells started ringing again, but louder and more raucous (rowdy, disorderly) than before.

The group instantly knew what this meant. Quasi, from his vantage point up in the bell tower, could clearly see what they could not: The dam had broken.

"Get out of the street!" Linus yelled, and his voice was so unexpectedly loud that people nearby felt shockwaves up their spines. The residents of Rickshaw Street who hadn't made it to higher ground yet now scrambled back into their homes or inside the nearest unlocked building and hurried up to the top floor.

Walter ran into the Kingscross School to make sure Madrigal and Clarice were all right. Ophelia accompanied her aunt and uncle into Seven Hills Better Books, with a crabby Mr. Birdwistell leading them inside. Realizing that Quasimodo was now all alone across the street, Linus ran toward the church, hoping he'd make it there before being swept away by the floodwaters that, judging by an ever-increasing rumbling sound, weren't far upriver.

Linus banged his fists against the locked door of the bell tower, yelling, "Quasi! Quasi! Hurry! Let me in! Open the door!"

The rumbling increased as the face of the flood barreled quickly toward Kingscross. In fact, Linus could now see the wall of rushing water rounding the elbow of the river upstream. It was white and fierce, faster and more powerful than anything he'd ever seen before.

twenty-three

Separated! And the Clock Is Ticking!

The door opened and a large arm, muscles straining, grabbed Linus's elbow and yanked him off his feet. Quasimodo slammed the door shut as he slung Linus over his shoulder and sped up the tower steps more quickly than his skinny legs had ever carried him before.

When they finally stood at the top, the face of the flood had passed by, and below them, small trees and a host of branches, as well as splintered wood and several garden sheds, floated past on the rushing, muddied waters of the Bard River.

"Thanks." Linus leaned against the wall, breathing heavily. He'd never felt a stab of fear like that in his life. All he could envision was being swept away, tumbling in the coils of water, getting caught on something under the flow, and ultimately drowning. His heart thundered beneath his breastbone.

"Thank these hearing aids," Quasi said modestly.

Quasimodo grabbed two ropes and began pulling again; the iron bells pealed their warning. Linus knew it was too late for anyone else to get to high ground now, but hopefully they were quick enough to make it to the upper stories of their houses.

He suppressed a smile. The Drs. Easterday thought themselves so adventuresome. Well, they had nothing on their kids!

Surely Ophelia and her aunt and uncle had garnered (gathered) the speed they needed. They stood at the kitchen window where the river—which now ran right past the shop leaving some of itself behind to ruin priceless books—carried more greenery and an old Volkswagen Beetle, bright blue, off to the west.

"The rain has stopped." Augustus laid aside the towel he'd retrieved from the bathroom and tried to arrange his hair with his fingers.

Portia began to cry. "My shop is ruined!"

It's one thing if a shopkeeper sells the latest clothing, CDs, toys, or anything that is easily replaced by a manufacturer who still makes those items (or others exactly like them). But Portia's stock was priceless. For instance, that original copy of *An Account of the Behaviour of Mr. James Maclaine, from the Time of his Condemnation to the Day of his Execution, October 3, 1750* published in 1750 by the Reverend Dr. Fifield Allen? There was no hopping on the Internet to order another one of those. Oh no! It might take Portia and Auggie years to fill up her bookshop once again.

"I even lost my new LED sign!" she wailed.

Augustus sat with his sister at the kitchen table, put his arm around her shoulders, and let her have a good cry. Augustus Sandwich knows how to let a person get it all out right when they need to.

Mr. Birdwistell, thankfully, was seated in the living room and snoring away like a moving train. His nose twitched every so often thanks to the dust that was still floating around from the uprooted carpet.

Ophelia knew she needed to get a move on and finish reading the book. So she gave her aunt a quick kiss and a loving caress on the cheek before hurrying down the hallway to her bedroom. At 7:00 a.m. the natural light was slim and the electricity nonexistent, thanks to the storm, so she slipped her flashlight out of her nightstand drawer and began reading.

Ten minutes later, Walter snuck into her room. "Everything's good at the school. I'm assuming they made it to higher ground."

"Good. I saw Clarice and Ms. Pierce leave the building. Now let me read."

"Right." He dropped to the floor and began doing push-ups.

Ophelia read as Quasimodo swept down and rescued Esmeralda from the gallows, gathered her in his arms, and climbed the face of the Cathedral of Notre-Dame as he cried out, "Sanctuary!"

Back in medieval times, churches were what is known as a place of sanctuary. In other words, people who needed protection could find it within those sacred walls. Quasimodo, knowing that Esmeralda was facing imminent (likely to occur very soon) execution for witchcraft, swung her into his sheltered world, hoping he could take care of her.

Oh, Quasi, Ophelia thought. *You'd still do this very act, wouldn't you? Even after being here in Real World with us. You'd never let someone hang who didn't deserve it.*

She wondered if what they'd done would save him in the end. She read on, gobbling up every word and looking for a place where, if she gave Quasi enough warning, he could change the course of his actions and save both Esmeralda and himself.

Her breathing quickened, her body became agitated, and her foot began rhythmically tapping against the bedspread. She barely noticed that the outside world had become brighter and the sun was now shining on the waters that muddied up most of Rickshaw Street, until Walter slid the flashlight out of her grasp and turned it off.

"I'm going to get you something to eat," he said. He paused and looked at her closely, examining her face. "We can help him, right? He doesn't have to meet his fate in quite the same way, does he?"

Ophelia looked up from the book and asked, "Have you read this?"

He nodded.

"So you know what happens?"

"Yeah. We've got to help him, Ophelia. We can't let him make those same mistakes. He's our friend. We have to warn him more specifically. When the Gypsy King and his men—"

"Don't ruin it for me!"

"PB&J?" he asked.

"Make that two. I'm starving."

At 9:30 a.m. the waters, only a few feet deep now, had finally slowed to a crawl. Walter turned away from the bedroom window. "Why isn't Linus bringing Quasi over here?"

Ophelia set her book on her lap. "He most likely can't swim."

"But the water's not that deep."

She got up and looked out. The flood flowed just underneath the windowsills on the first floor. "I wonder how long it's going to take for them to subside?"

Walter shrugged. "I've never met with this sort of thing before."

"Me either." Ophelia sighed. "But I doubt it'll be before 11:11."

"I'd say that's a safe guess."

Walter knew getting Quasi over to the house would be a big enough challenge, but how to sneak him upstairs with the aunt and uncle around? And that cranky Birdwistell, too. He was going to be a problem.

"I'm headed over to the church," he said. "We should at least see if they're all right."

"Oh!" Ophelia sat up straight. "I was so worried about finishing this book, I didn't even consider that Linus might not have made it into the church before the flood!"

"You would have known in your heart if he hadn't," said Walter. "Twins are connected like that, right?"

She nodded. "It's the best thing about it."

Walter left the room. Having a brother or sister, extra-special wordless connection or not, would have been the best thing he could have imagined.

Maybe twin friends will suffice, he thought, hoping that once this crazy adventure came to a close, Linus and Ophelia would still want to hang out with him. They would, wouldn't they?

Stop worrying, Walter, he chided himself. Just do what you have to do right now. You can cross that bridge when you come to it.

Speaking of bridges, with all of that filthy, disgusting water pooled at the foot of the stairs, not to mention lots and lots of books (which were already smelly, if you'll recall) floating around, Walter could have used one.

He descended the final few steps, and the water enveloped him to the top of his thighs as he went.

Upstairs, Ophelia heard footsteps overhead. She looked toward the ceiling, knowing those small thumps came from the attic. It can't be Linus and Quasi. There's no way they would have crossed Rickshaw Street and gone from the bell tower straight into the attic! Neither was that foolhardy. She knew Walter had just left the house, and Aunt Portia and Uncle Auggie still knew nothing about the hidden laboratory. And she could hear Birdwistell down in the kitchen complaining about the lack of nine-grain bread for his midmorning toast.

Only thirty pages and sixty minutes left to go, so Ophelia decided she could take no chances. Frollo and Cato could just lump it if that's who was up there. Quasi was in no danger as long as he was over at the church—

Oh no! Walter!

Ophelia hurried to the window, but she couldn't see Walter. He must have made it across. Boys like Walter always make it across.

Should I follow him? she wondered. But then she decided that reading was the most important thing she had to do right now. If she failed to finish the book before 11:11, then Quasimodo would expire painfully. The rest of it? Well, they'd just have to make everything up as they went along.

twenty-four

Really, Surviving a Flash Flood Should Be Enough Trouble for One Day

Dripping all over the stone steps, Walter banged on the door of the church figuring that Quasi and Linus had probably evacuated the bell tower in search of some place a little more comfortable.

Linus opened the door a minute later. "Walt! Is Ophelia okay?"

"Absolutely. Reading like crazy." He removed his shoes and stepped into the church.

The sanctuary, thankfully, sat higher than ground level. "Looks good in here," he said, jamming his hands in his pockets.

"The classrooms downstairs are practically flooded to the ceiling," Quasi said mournfully, obviously tenderhearted when it came to church buildings.

Walter sat down on the back pew and raked a hand through his hair. "I feel sorry for Father Lou when he gets back. He'll sure need us to lend him a hand."

"So will my aunt and uncle and Ms. Pierce." With the toe of his shoe, Linus traced a stone that helped pave the aisle.

Quasi said, "I wish I could stay. I'd be a big help."

Nobody doubted that. No one who had the pleasure of meeting Quasimodo wanted him to return to France; each of his newfound friends wished with all their hearts that he could remain a part of their lives in Kingscross.

"We've got to get you two back to the bookshop," said Walter.

"Quasi's a little worried about crossing the river."

Quasimodo nodded. "Sorry about that. I've just never—"

"Say no more," said Walter. "We'll figure something out. Wait. Linus, you're a building genius, right? Surely you can find something we can use to build a raft, can't you?"

Linus nodded. Now, that I can do.

Frollo frowned as he sat on the blue couch and drummed his fingers along the cording that edged the cushion. "You're certain you can get us through this circle as soon as we get Quasimodo inside of it?"

Cato sighed as he thumbed through one of his tomes, this one spelling out the importance of proper hygiene when traveling by circle. Obviously the author had a personal ax to grind, as nine times out of ten Cato traveled between worlds without a shower. *(You can be certain that I try to steer clear of Cato as much as possible.)*

"Relatively sure," he said.

Frollo reddened. "That's not good enough."

"You, sir, have nothing to say about it. Simply put, you are at my mercy. How does that feel?"

Cato had read *The Hunchback of Notre-Dame* in college. Quite frankly, he didn't care for Frollo any more than Ophelia did. Knowing of Frollo's eventual demise was the only thing that enabled him to stomach the self-righteous clergyman. Besides, the man was highly annoying.

Frollo said nothing.

Cato checked his watch. "It's 10:30 a.m. Forty-one minutes left."

"And here we are, just waiting for them to come to us. I don't like it," said Frollo. "This is incompetence at its finest. If I were in charge—"

"Ah, but you're not," said Cato. "So if I were you, I'd do myself a favor and remain quiet. We don't want to be discovered too soon."

"But what if they don't come to the attic?"

"They will. They'd never let something terrible happen to Quasimodo." He tilted his chin and glared up at Frollo. "Unlike you."

Cato was of a mind to usher Quasimodo into the world of a completely different book, deposit Frollo right into the middle of an ensuing witchcraft trial, and do Quasimodo the favor of his life.

But he hadn't perfected the process yet, and who knew what would happen to the young hunchback if Cato gave it a try?

Ophelia shut the book with tears in her eyes and fear in her heart. Oh, what a sad ending! Quasi didn't deserve to go that way—and all for the love of a fickle young woman who was, Ophelia couldn't help but say it, not the sharpest tack on the bulletin board.

She picked up a notepad and a pen. Across the top of the sheet, she quickly wrote:

Things You Need to Know.

Ophelia gave not a single hoot that by warning Quasi, she might change the course of literary history all over the world, rendering reading guides and books and dissertations as exercises in lunacy. She cared only about Quasimodo. Ending up so sad and alone? He deserved none of that. She simply wouldn't allow it.

The bedside clock read 10:46 a.m.

Twenty-five more minutes.

Linus placed the crude raft that he'd formed from a plastic playhouse onto the church steps. The cheerful yellow siding, pink door, and blue shutters were in stark contrast against the somber, brown tones of the muddy river.

Quasimodo eyed it suspiciously. "You want me to climb up on that thing?"

Linus nodded.

"It'll be fine," said Walter. "Just climb on and Linus and I will pull you across."

"I don't know," he said, doubt underlining his words.

"Let's go," said Linus. "Only twenty minutes left until the circle is open."

In other words, there was no time to argue.

Quasimodo gingerly climbed onto the raft, which was no trouble at all for someone who could scale walls, and looked back at them. "Now I feel a little stupid."

"Don't," said Walter, casting off. "We don't know what we would have done without you."

"I wonder if we can call you back another time?" Linus asked as they waded through the chest-high water.

Quasimodo jerked his head higher and looked back at him. "Do you think the book will say?"

"We'll ask Ophelia." With a heavy heart, Linus pushed the playhouse raft across the stream.

"Come on, come on, come on," Ophelia whispered as she stared out the bedroom window. Then she saw the odd group making its way toward the house. She ran down the steps as quietly as she could so as not to alert Cato and Frollo of her presence. She checked on Aunt Portia and Uncle Augustus.

Birdwistell, thankfully, had left the house in a huff, wondering what kind of people were satisfied living their lives without orange marmalade.

There in the living room, her uncle was asleep on the couch, his knees curled toward the back of the furniture, his thin spine— its bumps parading down the length of his pajama top—facing her. Snoring. Good.

Aunt Portia had taken to her bed, a pale blue satin sleeping mask over her eyes. Ophelia held her breath and listened. Her aunt usually slept like someone who'd danced in an all-night dance-a-thon. (Portia actually does that sort of thing, you know.) Great. And no wonder. Running up and down the street and yelling in the dark would most certainly have taken it out of people their age, no matter how well preserved they were.

By the time Ophelia reached the staircase that led into the bookshop, the guys were helping Quasimodo off the raft. And then the three of them waded through the shop.

"Bad news," she whispered. "Cato and Frollo are upstairs. They want to get Quasi and take him back through Cato's other circle, which means it must not be far away."

"What are we going to do?" asked Walter.

"I've got a plan."

twenty-five

The Smartest People Are Sometimes the Easiest to Fool

I wonder how many novel chapters have ended with the statement, "I've got a plan?" Probably more than we wish to consider. This time-worn, yet wonderfully effective device is known as a "hook." Utilizing a hook, the author begs the reader to ask himself a rather consuming question—in this case, "How are they going to get rid of those two ne'er-do-wells (idle, worthless people) and get Quasimodo back into the circle before the acids between the two worlds dissolve him?"—and desire an answer right away. The page is turned; the story continues. Bravo!

Let's find out, shall we? Ophelia is quite the planner.

They said their good-byes before putting the plan in motion.

Walter shook Quasi's hand. "It's been nice knowing you, mate. Sorry to see you go."

Quasi covered their clasped hands with his free one and squeezed. "You're a good lad, Walter. Keep on the up and up. You won't be sorry."

Their eyes met, and Walter wondered how in the world Quasimodo knew who he really was—or more precisely, who he'd once been.

Linus offered his hand to Quasi next. They shook, and then Quasi drew him into a quick, strong embrace, saying, "Take good care of Ophelia. She's special. And you're not so bad yourself, Linus. If only you didn't talk so much."

They pulled apart.

"Will do," said Linus. "Be careful back there. Make us proud." He cleared his throat.

And finally, Ophelia stepped forward. They put their arms around each other. "You've been such a good friend," Quasi said.

"You too. I'm going to miss you." She bit back the tears.

She handed him the list of instructions she'd drawn up earlier. "If you don't want to end up the way Victor Hugo said you would, read this when you get back. I'm hoping—" she crossed her fingers "—that we can at least change your future, Quasi, even if it's just for that one copy of the book that you're in."

"I hope so too." All color drained from his face. "I wish I didn't have to go."

"So do we," said Walter.

"Maybe you can bring me through again sometime, or at least give it a try?" A look of hope softened his face.

Ophelia nodded. "I don't see why we can't at least try."

"So," said Walter, who hated good-byes more than anybody else in the room did, "this is really more of a 'see you later' than a 'good-bye forever.'"

"I guess so," said Ophelia, brightening.

"Sounds good to me," Quasimodo laughed.

"Then let's do this," said Linus.

Eight minutes left.

Obviously they couldn't say a flood was coming. The Bard River Dam had already made sure of that. No, Ophelia's plan was a little less consuming.

She hurried up the attic stairs and burst into the room, slamming the door into the wall behind it with a loud bang.

Frollo jumped.

"Good heavens!" cried Cato. "Couldn't you at least knock?"

Well, it was his attic, really. I suppose he had a right to say that, in a strange sort of way.

"I need your help!" Ophelia cried.

Cato crossed his arms and raised a perfect eyebrow. "Oh, yes?"

"Quasimodo's still across the street. How far away is your circle?"

"My dear, I don't need a circle anymore." His mouth turned down.

Frollo glared at him. "Didn't you just say—"

"Oh be quiet, man," said Cato. "Why would I divulge all of my secrets to you?"

"You need to go get him, then, and get him back to Paris before he fizzles. He will fizzle, right?"

"Yes."

"But can you take him back?"

"It's risky," Cato shot a glance at Frollo, "but I think it will work."

Ophelia gestured toward the door. "Then you'd better go. He's still in the bell tower, I think. Or he might be in the sanctuary."

Frollo startled at that word.

"Oh, don't worry," said Cato, turning to the deacon. "It just describes the room of a church. It's not a place where people can find refuge. It's not like that anymore."

Frollo looked like he didn't know whether to laugh or cry about that.

"Hurry! You have only a couple of minutes left now!" Ophelia cried, pushing Cato toward the door.

Frollo barged his way through, exiting the attic first.

Ophelia grabbed Cato's arm. "Frollo won't make good on his promises. You know that, don't you?"

"I do," Cato said. "If Quasimodo doesn't do anything stupid because of Esmeralda, then he's my next best bet to get that emerald necklace."

"The Gypsy king is an even better bet."

Cato shook his head and shrugged, mystified.

"You haven't read the book?" she gasped.

"Not in years. And when I say years, Ophelia, I mean more years than you might think."

"My advice?" said Ophelia. "Put Frollo in right before Quasimodo reappears in the stocks. They'll get him for witchcraft for sure."

"It'll be easier to get them both back at the same time anyway. It will be so nice to be rid of that man. What a royal pain he turned out to be."

Ophelia looked at the clock on the wall. Less than two minutes left now. "Hurry!"

Cato winked at her. "Oh, I think it'll be all right. I know Quasimodo is here. Do you have the right page for the transfer?"

"Yes."

"Good."

He disappeared down the steps. Ophelia grabbed the backpack of goodies she'd prepared for Quasimodo.

"Come on, you guys!" she hissed, knowing the last thing they needed was for Aunt Portia and Uncle Augustus to awaken just then.

She looked around her. The book! Where was the book?

The group entered the attic with thirty seconds left to go. "I can't find the book," she said, her voice rising in intensity.

"Get in the circle, Quasi," said Walter. "Maybe the book doesn't have to be there."

"But Cato said—"

Ophelia spun around, her eyes searching.

The room began to rumble. Quasimodo, now clutching his bag of treats, looked paler than a snowman, but bravely he stepped inside the circle. The circle glowed. Ophelia felt sick. What if she'd failed him? What if he melted in pain and agony? She'd never forgive herself.

"Just think hard, Quasi. Will yourself to enter a few minutes after you disappeared!"

"I'll try!"

Then she saw the book, stuck between the sofa cushions. She grabbed it and tossed it in. It landed facedown. Whatever page it was opened to was now left to fate.

Then, like it had at 11:11 p.m. just sixty hours before, the circle glowed in rainbow hues. The wooden bird took flight and settled on Quasi's head. Sparks shot up around the perimeter casting a violent white light that left a green circle on their retinas after it had died down, and Quasimodo, waving a hand, disappeared.

twenty-six

Back to Boring Old Summer — Don't You Just Feel So Sorry for Them?

"Well," said Walter, "I suppose the portal will open once again on the eleventh of next month?"

Ophelia sat down on the blue couch. "Yep. Funny how all the wooden carvings disappeared, isn't it?"

"I guess once the portal is opened, strange things can happen until it's closed again."

"What about the food?" asked Linus.

"Cato," Ophelia and Walter said simultaneously.

"But how?"

Ophelia shrugged. "I think a lot of this remains to be seen, don't you?"

Linus threw himself down next to her as Walter dropped and did some sit-ups.

"So?" asked Walter. "In a month from now, the summer's sure to be pretty boring, don't you think? Another adventure would be brilliant."

Ophelia crossed her legs beneath her. "I don't know, Walt. I've been thinking about that." She reached over to the side table for a PB&J, and then looked at it wistfully. "I miss Quasi so much. Maybe it's better not to bring people forward. It hurts too much when they go back."

True, thought Linus who fondly remembered Quasi up in a tree with Kyle. He could have done so much good around Kingscross. Hopefully Paris won't be the same after Quasi's return.

Ophelia returned the sandwich to the plate. Oh dear. Too many of them in three days' time, and now her favorite snack was ruined.

"But isn't it worth it?" Walter stood to his feet, eyes sparkling. "Think about it, Ophelia. We got to know and love the hunchback of Notre-Dame! Personally! How many people in the world can say such a thing? And what's more, we have the opportunity to get to know others. Who in their right mind would turn down something like this?"

Ophelia stood to her feet. "You know what? You're right, Walter. You're exactly right! Why wouldn't we?"

Uh-oh, thought Linus.

"I'll go to my bookshelf right now."

Linus put himself between Ophelia and the attic door. "Be careful. Quasi was a good guy. Maybe you should try and make sure—"

"Make sure, nothing!" cried Walter. "Give us the adventure of our lives, Ophelia. Make what we did with Quasimodo nothing short of a walk in the park."

"Are you crazy?" Linus turned to him.

Walter grabbed half a sandwich, bit down, and then smiled, shoving the bite into his cheek with his tongue. "Yes, mate. I certainly am."

Ophelia stood before her bookshelf, her arms crossed in front of her. It was an easy pick as far as she was concerned—especially considering the theme of Uncle Auggie's next party. And it was a book she'd been wanting to read for a good long time. But she needed to get started right away. Some writers have no idea when to stop, you see, and Herman Melville surely fit that description with his long-winded classic (which you shall most likely have to read in high school or college).

Moby-Dick.

Ophelia hurried back up the steps and handed the book to her brother, who then read the title to himself and handed the book to Walter.

"Let's just hope the whale doesn't show up, or we'll be in real trouble," said Walter.

"Captain Ahab could do his fair share of damage too," said

Ophelia, who was well aware of the seaman's obsession with finding and killing the great white whale who'd taken his leg.

Linus sighed and continued tinkering with Cato Grubbs's lab equipment. He'd made no real discovery yet, but the burner sure kept Ronda's queso dip warm. "You'd better get started reading then."

A look of boredom settled over Walter's features. "What do you say we head over to the camp and see the kids, Linus?"

Ophelia waved them away, her eyes capturing the first line of *Moby-Dick*.

"Call me Ishmael."

Well, okay. I certainly will, she giggled to herself and began consuming a whale of a tale.

Thus ends the tale—or all the bits worth telling, mind you. They did sleep, use the bathroom, change clothing, and participate in mindless conversations. But a good writer leaves those bits out, usually, as they are boring and add nothing to the movement of the plot or the development of the character—the two most important considerations while writing a story. As one writer put it, "I leave out the boring bits."

One might say my little asides would fit that description too. But this is my book and I shall write it how I like. And now, I'm off to bed with a glass of juice and a bowl of potato chips. And you … well, please don't disturb me; I have quite a busy day ahead of me in the English department. Those professors still don't appreciate all that I do for them. But tomorrow the sun will rise, and those stuffy colleagues of mine might actually see the true worth of a literary fussbudget like myself.

Good night, good day, and good heavens! Go outside and do something with your body! You can't sit around reading all day.

the end

DISCARD

We want to hear from you. Please send your comments
about this book to us in care of zreview@zondervan.com. Thank you.

ZONDERVAN.com/
AUTHORTRACKER